Quest
for the
White Bull

Also by Don Coldsmith

THE SPANISH BIT SAGA:
   FORT DE CHASTAIGNE
   SONG OF THE ROCK
   TRAIL FROM TAOS
   THE FLOWER IN THE MOUNTAINS
   THE MEDICINE KNIFE
   RETURN TO THE RIVER
   RIVER OF SWANS
   PALE STAR
   THE SACRED HILLS
   MOON OF THUNDER
   DAUGHTER OF THE EAGLE
   MAN OF THE SHADOWS
   FOLLOW THE WIND
   THE ELK-DOG HERITAGE
   BUFFALO MEDICINE
   TRAIL OF THE SPANISH BIT
   THE CHANGING WIND—A Spanish Bit Super
    Edition

RIVERS WEST:
   THE SMOKY HILL

Quest for the White Bull

》》 》》 》》 》》 》》 》》 》》 》》 》》 》》 》》 》》 》》

DON COLDSMITH

A Double D Western
Doubleday

NEW YORK LONDON TORONTO SYDNEY AUCKLAND

A Double D Western
PUBLISHED BY DOUBLEDAY
a division of Bantam Doubleday Dell Publishing Group, Inc.
666 Fifth Avenue, New York, New York 10103

A Double D Western, Doubleday,
and the portrayal of the letters DD
are the trademarks of Doubleday, a division of
Bantam Doubleday Dell Publishing Group, Inc.

Library of Congress Cataloging-in-Publication Data

Coldsmith, Don, 1926–
    Quest for the white bull/Don Coldsmith.—1st ed.
        p.   cm.—(A Double D western)
    "Spanish bit saga book 17"—
        1. Indians of North America—Great Plains—Fiction.   I. Title.
II. Series.
PS3553.O445Q4   1990
813'.54—dc20   90-3163
CIP

W

ISBN 0-385-26301-5
Copyright © 1990 by Don Coldsmith
All Rights Reserved
Printed in the United States of America
November 1990
First Edition
BG

Time period: Early 1700s, a few years after *Fort de Chastaigne*

Quest
for the
White Bull

1
>> >> >>

The Sun Dance was not the usual enthusiastic celebration that summer. The triumphant symbolism of
the renewal of the sun, the grass, and the buffalo was
missing. Rather than prayers of thanks, the People
voiced prayers of supplication and entreaty.

For the buffalo had not returned. It had been suspected, at the time of last season's Fall Hunt, that
something was wrong. There had been a period of
unusual weather, cool when it should have been hot,
and wet when the dry season should have been expected. The Moon of Thunder, named for Rain Maker's noisy drums and the accompanying spears of real-
fire, had been virtually silent. Therefore, there had
been very little of the life-giving moisture to stimulate
the growth of the grasses. The Red Moon, following
next, should have been hot and dry but had instead
produced heavy rains, one after another. The rains
were welcomed, and the grass did return in its fall

glory, sending seed heads up toward the sun. But the growth had been strange, heavy but short.

And the buffalo knew. The herds came, migrating from the north, but they were scattered, and their behavior was unpredictable. The Fall Hunt was only fair. Most lodges managed to store enough for the winter, but there was a general feeling that something was not right. It was not known how far these conditions extended, until the Sun Dance the following year.

By previous arrangement, the People began to gather at Head-Split Creek in the Moon of Roses for the annual festival. It was only then that the widespread seriousness of the situation was discovered. The Eastern band had seen few buffalo at all and had resorted to hunting deer, like their neighbors of the forests. The Northern and Southern bands had managed, by long and hard effort, to store enough meat for the winter. The Mountain band and the Red Rocks, in the far western ranges of the People, had probably felt the impact of the problem least of all. Their area, against the eastern slopes of the mountains, presented different patterns of weather, different patterns of migration. Yet even they, the bands of the western plains and the foothills, had seen a change. There was a different mood, an uncomfortable change in the spirit of the grassland.

As the People gathered for the Sun Dance, various rumors flew and various theories emerged. The old women clucked their tongues and predicted dire events, blaming the Council for poor management. It was not clear how the Council was at fault. There were, of course, traditionalists who insisted that the situation was a result of departure from the old ways. There was far too much use, these reactionaries insisted, of the medicine of the whites. Many of the People now built fires with flint and steel instead of with rubbing-sticks. The ultra-conservatives even objected to the use of metal knives, but the usefulness of such implements outweighed any risks, for most.

There was always someone to blame for misfortune. A whispered campaign began to place responsibility on the medicine men of the People. If they had been alert to the demands of their positions, would they not have foreseen this problem and taken steps to guide the People away from it?

White Fox, the eldest holy man of the tribe, was only too aware of these mutterings. Was it not he, some were asking, who had participated in the attempt by the French to explore the River of the Kenzas a few summers ago? Surely, that had ended in disaster. This criticism came at an inopportune time. His was the responsibility to announce the formal opening of the Sun Dance. His son and assistant, young Red Horse, would accompany him, marching four times daily around the encampment for three days. Horse would beat cadence on the medicine drum while White Fox, wearing the elk-dog medicine around his neck, held the Sun Doll aloft and chanted the announcement.

However, the Sun Dance lodge was not ready. The brush arbor had been prepared, but one thing was missing, the effigy of the buffalo. This part of the preparation was the responsibility of the family of Six Elk, Real-chief of the People. Elk's young men had searched the prairie in vain. They must find the largest, most noble buffalo bull available for the ceremonies. The skin would be stretched over a framework of brush and poles in a lifelike pose, with the intact head facing the rising sun across the dance arena. It was a matter of pride to obtain an outstanding specimen. This had never presented a problem before.

But this season, no buffalo were to be found. Not only was there no outstanding specimen, the scouts reported, there were none at all. Not one mangy old cow. Publicly, Six Elk's family tried to keep up the pretense of careful selection of the Sun Dance Bull. Privately, they had conceded that *any* buffalo would have to suffice. The Real-chief had confided as much to White Fox. Their shared problem was obvious. The formal announcements of the Sun Dance, lasting three days, could not begin until the bull was available.

The People were growing restless. The excitement of visiting relatives and renewing old friendships seemed flat and uninteresting in the face of present problems. There was some racing and gambling, but these activities, too, lacked excitement. A sense of foreboding overshadowed the entire camp.

White Fox sought desperately for some way to break out of this impasse. He had chanted and prayed and cast the bones but was receiving no clear answers. His concern became greater, and he sought comfort in consultation with his wife, South Wind.

"What more can I do, Wind?" he asked. "You have a feel for such things."

She shrugged. "I do not know, my husband. What does Red Horse say?"

He thought a little while before answering. Their son had married three seasons ago and was living in his own lodge. Though he had learned rapidly as an apprentice, and showed great insight, he was, after all, still an apprentice. White Fox shook his head.

"He does not have the experience, the maturity, Wind."

"But you could ask him," she insisted. "You had less experience when you took your vision-quest and found me."

"Yes, that is true," he said thoughtfully. "But there are those with more experience."

"Of course!" South Wind said eagerly. "Could you ask the other holy men to meet with you?"

"Maybe . . . I do not know, Wind. It is not usual. They have their medicine, as I have mine. These are different gifts."

"Yes, I know. But Fox, you have told me . . . in Looks Far's day, did not the holy men of different tribes once work together?"

"Why, yes, they did," he answered in surprise. "There was the threat of the Blue Paints. Looks Far, with his buffalo medicine, and the Head Splitter holy man—Wolf's Head, I think—the two worked together. Their medicines helped each other, wolf and buffalo."

"Then why not ask?"

"Yes . . . yes, that is good, Wind."

In a very short time, Red Horse was busily circulating among the bands of the encampment. It was not a public announcement, just a quiet request to each holy man—or, more properly, holy person. There was one medicine woman in the Eastern band, said to be very good with herbs. The people notified were merely invited to the lodge of White Fox after sundown, to sit, smoke, and talk.

They gathered quietly, fully aware of the reason for this unusual council: Night-Walker, the owl prophet from the Northern band; Cat Woman, the herb doctor; Plenty Snows, from the far foothills, and his apprentice, Lost Calf. The Red Rocks were without a holy man at present, but the newly widowed wife of old Seeks-Eagles was present. She had been his assistant for many years, and it was said that he had bequeathed her his gift from his deathbed. That remained to be seen, of course.

White Fox lighted the pipe, blew smoke to the four directions, and lifted it aloft before passing it on to his left. Not a word was said as the instrument made its round. When finally it was returned to White Fox, he knocked the dottle into his palm and tossed it into the fire. Then he handed the pipe to Red Horse, who ceremoniously replaced it in its decorated case.

"My friends," Fox began, "you know why we are here."

There were nods of agreement, and Fox continued.

"This is a matter more serious than any in our lifetime."

More nods, and a murmur went round the circle, indicating an understanding of the crisis that now faced the People.

"Six Elk tells me that his young men have seen no buffalo at all."

"This is true," said the owl prophet, whose Northern band was the home of the Real-chief's family. "My nephew is one of the hunters. There are no herds to be found."

"It is because the People have forgotten the old ways!" stated Cat Woman emphatically. "Look at your own moccasins, Night-Walker. They are decorated with *beads*, not quills!"

The owl prophet drew himself up indignantly. "And you cut your food with a metal knife," he retorted.

There was a murmur around the circle, and more accusations flew. White Fox held up his hands for silence.

"Stop, stop, my friends. Above all, we must not

quarrel. I have called us here to work together, not to argue."

"But we must agree on the cause," insisted the herb woman, "before we can correct it. The cause is that we have forgotten our roots!"

"What say you others?" Fox said quickly, to forestall a breakdown in the council. "Snows, you have not spoken."

The man from the Mountain band shrugged and was silent a moment, while the others waited.

"I do not know," he said at last. "Maybe the coming of new ways has had its effect. But at what point? Cat Woman mentions glass beads, Walker says metal knives. I have heard some say that the firestarters are bad."

He paused, but it was apparent that he had not finished.

"When we think of it," he mused, "what was the *first* change from old ways?"

The others looked questioningly at each other. What was the man trying to say?

"What do you mean, Snows?" demanded Cat Woman.

"I am not sure, except—have there not always been changes? Some better than others?"

An argumentative murmur erupted, but White Fox quieted it.

"This is true," he observed. "How far back does change begin? When the People crawled through the log into the world from inside the earth? That was a change from darkness."

Lost Calf giggled and drew a sharp look of reprimand from his teacher. Cat Woman bristled.

"You are being ridiculous," she accused. "If this is not to be serious, I will leave."

"No, no, sister. We search for truth and reason," Plenty Snows pleaded. "Continue, White Fox."

"I . . . I had no other thought," Fox said, slightly embarrassed. "But it seems we are asking, *When* did this begin?"

"When the pale-skinned ones came," Cat Woman accused. *"That* is when!"

"But Cat Woman," Plenty Snows said, in tones that were almost pleading, "they brought the horse. The First Horse, of the Southern band. Look, White Fox wears the elk-dog medicine bit on his neck! That medicine and the medicine of the buffalo have worked together! It has made the People rich and powerful."

"But at what loss?" snapped Cat Woman. She would never back away from her chosen ideas.

The owl prophet spoke. "That was long ago, many lifetimes. There must be something else. Have we forgotten something from our past?"

"Yes!" Cat Woman almost screeched at him. *"You* have!"

"Let us not argue," White Fox said firmly. "What did you mean, Night-Walker?"

"Again, I am not sure. It seems likely that we have each searched separately for an answer. We have prayed, burned our incense, asked our spirit-guides, cast our bones, whatever. But no one has answers. Could we all try at once?"

"You mean together?" asked Plenty Snows.

"No, maybe not, but at the same time. Tonight. All ask for their own help and meet again tomorrow night."

There were tentative nods of agreement. Then the widow from the Red Rocks, she of questionable credentials, spoke for the first time. She spoke to White

Fox, hesitantly, not wishing to be too forward or to offend.

"Tell us, Uncle, are there not the Story Skins?"

The others looked at one another in amazement. In their preoccupation with their own special problems, they had forgotten the pictographic record of the People.

"Yes!" Plenty Snows exclaimed. "May we study the Skins for answers, Uncle?"

The sudden use of the term of respect, "Uncle," reflected the prestige that White Fox held as custodian of the Story Skins. They had been handed down for generations, from one holy man to another, no one knew how long. There were gaps in the continuity. A skin or two had been lost or destroyed over the centuries, through fire, flood, or war, but most of the story remained intact. Usually there was one pictograph for each year, an account of the most important events in the history of the People.

"Of course!" agreed White Fox. "The light is poor now, but let us start. Then we can call on our spirit-guides tonight and come back in the light of day."

He reached behind the lodge lining and drew out several long, rolled cylinders. He selected one and untied the thongs to unroll the skin on the floor of the lodge.

"This is the most recent skin," he explained. "Then we can go backward."

The others gathered around to study the story of the People.

2

>> >> >>

Red Horse gathered with the others around the unfurled pictographs. He had seen the Story Skins before, of course. In fact, as a child he had watched in fascinated silence as his father painstakingly added the year's new pictures. His mother had cautioned him to silence.

"This is a thing of great importance," South Wind had reminded him. "It is one of the greatest responsibilities of the holy man. You may watch, but not a word, now!"

Years later, as an apprentice, he had watched the procedure and had assisted by grinding and mixing the pigments for his father. Some day, the keeping of the Story Skins would be his responsibility, as he assumed the duties of his father's position as holy man.

But now, by the flickering light of the fire in his parents' lodge, there seemed to be a new thrill, an excitement in the air. The holy ones from all the bands were gathered, searching for answers to the problems of the People. He could not have said why, but he had a feeling that the answer was to be found here, in the old stories of the tribe.

There were murmurs from the group, as they identified past events. There, only a few seasons ago, was depicted the explosion of the French fort, de Chastaigne. He had witnessed it. *Aiee*, how frightening . . . like a thousand spears of real-fire! But now—

"Look!" said someone. "The first trading trip to Santa Fe, for metal knives!"

That had been carried out by ancestors of Red Horse. He had heard stories of the troubles the first trading parties encountered. And the last trip had been disastrous. His father, White Fox, had been in great danger on that one. The pueblo tribes had risen up, to chase the Spanish out of their area. What . . . yes! His grandfather, Red Feather, had married a woman of that area. *Her* parents had not participated in the war and had come home with the People from the plains. Had he not heard that his family still had pueblo relatives living on the upper River of the Kenzas?

His thoughts returned to the present. They must go back farther in the People's story. White Fox was tracing the spiral of the years backward, toward the center of the skin.

"Here is an important event." He pointed. "The destruction of the Blue Paint invaders. See, our ancestor, Looks Far, joins with Wolf's Head, the Head Splitter holy man, to bring it about."

The picture was graphic. Large numbers of armed warriors, their faces marked with blue, were being pushed over a cliff by stampeding herds of buffalo. He had heard this story many times.

"Maybe that is it!" cried Cat Woman. "We should not be allied with Head Splitters!"

Several looked at her with disgust. It appeared that the woman would have a negative reaction to anything that was mentioned.

"But," White Fox noted gently, "the People have prospered greatly from that alliance."

The spiraling pictographs, followed backward through the generations, ended in the center of the skin, and White Fox rerolled it.

"This is the next one back," he stated. "An important one. . . . It shows the coming of the horse."

There, plainly depicted for the first time in the Story Skins, was a warrior riding on a horse, holding a long spear and impaling a running buffalo.

"Who is the man?" asked Lost Calf in awe.

"An ancestor of ours," White Fox said proudly. "An outsider. See the fur upon his face, and the strange roundness of his head? He brought this, the elk-dog medicine, by which we control the horse."

He pointed to the Spanish bit, worn as an amulet around his own neck.

"What is the matter with his head?" asked Lost Calf.

"He was called Heads Off," Fox explained. "He became a sub-chief of the People, because of his skill with elk-dogs. It is said that he could remove his head."

There were gasps of disbelief.

"See this picture?" Fox pointed. "His name is shown, so."

The individuals in the pictographs were identified by a line from their figure, leading to a circle indicating the person's name. Red Horse identified a battle scene depicting Heads Off striking down an enemy who was apparently named Gray Wolf.

"I am made to think he did not really remove his head," White Fox was explaining. "Maybe it was a round headdress, of a type not seen now."

The others nodded, studying the pictures of this remarkable man.

Red Horse was thinking of something else. His attention was fixed on an even earlier picture. It too depicted a stampede of buffalo over a steep bluff. But they were being driven by men *on foot*. This was before the time of the First Horse. He squinted harder in the flickering light, trying to make out a figure who seemed to be in the midst of the stampede, right at the cliff's edge. Who was this very brave man? Horse traced the line from the man's chest to the identifying circle above it. The head of a buffalo . . . a *white* buffalo.

"Who is this man, Uncle?" he asked his father, using the term of respect in the presence of others.

"Oh, that is long ago," White Fox pointed out. "Before the coming of Heads Off and the elk-dogs. He was a holy man . . . White Buffalo."

Fox turned to answer someone else's question.

Red Horse sat staring at the figure on the painted skin. His attention continued to be drawn there. Somehow, he felt a kinship of the spirit with this young man of long ago. He looked for other pictographs of the holy man White Buffalo, and he found them. There had been at least two such men, it seemed, father and son. In some of the pictures, one or the other was depicted in a cape of white fur, with the upper part a horned headdress. A cape made of the skin of a white buffalo!

But what had happened to this man of great medicine? Horse could almost feel the mystical powers of this holy man. He must have been extremely impor-

tant to the People, because he appeared several times.
He had played a part in reconciling the new medicine
of the elk-dog with that of the buffalo. Yes, their signs
appeared together for a few seasons, then no more. He
was sure that the buffalo medicine had continued, together with that of the horse. He had been required to
study and practice it as an apprentice. But after a
certain point in the spiral, there were no more pictographs identifying White Buffalo. Obviously, the man
had crossed over. But after his death would not someone have assumed his duties and the possession of the
cape? He leaned over to study the time period involved. It was difficult, because that portion of the
spiral was on the side opposite him and therefore upside down.

Ah, there . . . a picture of a man wearing the cape!
But wait . . . this man was identified by two dogs in
his name circle. And—*aiee,* Horse had not realized,
because the picture was upside down—this man, Two
Dogs, was wearing the white cape, but it was dirty and
torn! Bloody, from the gore that gushed from his belly.

So, a man called Two Dogs had been killed by a
buffalo while wearing the cape. The cape itself must
have been destroyed, because it did not appear again.
How had it happened? And why did the wearer of the
cape, which had been so important to the People,
expose it to such an event? Such a risk? It appeared
that this had been a significant loss to the tribe's spiritual life.

There was another figure in that same pictograph, a
man called simply Owl. This man seemed to have
been injured but had apparently recovered, because
he appeared in later pictures. It also seemed that he
was a holy man, one well respected. But he had never
worn the skin of the white buffalo.

Red Horse lay awake a long time that night. Blue Swallow did not question him, because she knew he was deeply disturbed over the problems of the People. When he returned from the council of holy ones at the lodge of his father, he had been very quiet. He had mentioned simply that everyone was to meditate and seek answers, each in his own medicine. She could tell that he had encountered something, some idea, and that he was working on it. This was how he behaved at such times.

They retired, and she snuggled close, but he remained preoccupied. Swallow slept, wakened, and slept again, and each time her husband was awake.

Red Horse's thoughts whirled in confusion. He was convinced that he had chanced upon something important. But what? Here was a mystery, generations old, that he could not decipher. A skilled medicine man, or maybe several generations of them, bearing the same name, White Buffalo. . . . A white cape, worn by the man or men who bore the name. What an exciting thing of the spirit! The People, taking spiritual guidance from a holy man with such a spectacular talisman.

And it had been lost—the cape, the name—destroyed. There appeared to have been a conflict between the two holy men in the pictograph. Had the survivor, Owl, overthrown the long-standing medicine of the white buffalo cape? It seemed not, because he was later depicted with honor. But it was plain that the cape itself had been destroyed, a tremendous loss.

Red Horse wrestled a long time with this, seeking sleep that would not come. It must have been near daylight before he became convinced of one basic premise. Somehow, he did not know how, the problems that the People were experiencing now were related to the loss of the white cape many generations ago.

He had not had a chance to speak with his father about it, but surely he would tomorrow. Meanwhile, if he could, he would sleep and seek the benefit to his inquiring spirit that the sleep might bring.

He sighed and turned over, trying not to disturb Swallow. He would tell her about his disturbing discovery, too. He told her about everything . . . only now, he was still so confused . . . what could he say?

Finally he drifted into a troubled sleep and began to dream. . . .

3

>> >> >>

Afterward, he was never certain whether it had been a night-dream or a thing of the spirit, like a vision-quest. He sometimes wondered if there was really any difference. It was not a thing to be explained, anyway, but to be experienced and nurtured. A thing of the spirit either way, perhaps.

Maybe it was because he had been thinking so hard before he slept, thinking of the Story Skins and of his ancestor White Buffalo and of the People. Whatever the reason, and whatever the means of its occurrence, what happened was so unnerving that his life was never the same. And neither, of course, was the life of the People.

Red Horse found himself riding across an open plain. It was like a dream, to be sure. However, it was the strange sort of dream that happens only rarely. The dreamer knows that it is a dream, and is observing it in a detached way, though still involved. Red Horse felt that he was riding across the plain and at the same time *watching* himself ride across the plain. Both sensations were quite real, as real as the feel of the horse's muscles against his knees, and the smell of the animal's sweat, and the scent of unfamiliar plants. Along with this was the feeling that, if he wished, he could waken. But he did not want to do so. His mission on the plain was exciting, important, and real. He was interested and involved, eager to see what would happen next.

The terrain was not that of the familiar tallgrass hills, the Sacred Hills of the People. The grass here was sparse and bunched. In some areas there were large expanses of the short, curly grass that the buffalo relish in early summer. In other areas, nothing seemed to grow at all, except rocks and sand and occasional stalks of yucca. It must be late summer, because the yucca was past bloom. Shiny green seedpods adorned the stalks.

Some would not have noted such detail in a dream, if dream this was. But Red Horse was a holy man, or at least a skilled apprentice. His instruction, his striving for the gifts of the spirit, had sharpened his powers of notice. The knowledge and observation of plants, animals, and the signs of earth and sky had become his life. And, in this strange dream state, he was able to think these thoughts and watch himself react according to the strict dictates of his father's teaching.

A coyote trotted from behind a clump of yucca, stopped, and squatted on its haunches a short bow shot away. The path of his horse would take him quite near the creature, but it made no effort to move. Coyotes were common here, as everywhere, apparently. He had heard them last night. *Last night . . . how could he have memories of last night as part of a dream?*

He rode on toward the animal, noting that his horse sniffed curiously, ears pricked forward. They had nearly reached the spot where the coyote squatted when the horse slowed and stopped. Impatient, he started to dig a heel into the horse's flank, but paused. Wait . . . something the horse knows . . . *aiee!* Of course. This was no ordinary coyote but his own spirit-guide. He should have known! He had overlooked that possibility, but his horse had recognized it immediately.

He was a bit embarrassed by this turn of events. He had neglected communication with his spirit-guide, maybe. Only a time or two since his vision-quest had he had occasion to make such contact. Now, his guide had come to him, implying great importance to this dream. More importance, it seemed, than any since his vision-quest, when he had found his spirit-guide. That signified in turn that this might be one of the most important events of his life. Gently, he kneed the horse closer and drew it to a stop. The animal made a soft snuffling noise toward the coyote, as if in greeting, and the coyote seemed to nod.

"Good day to you, Uncle," Red Horse greeted. "I am glad to see you."

He was nervous, wondering if he was to be reprimanded for neglecting contact with his guide. But he had really had no need until now, and Grandfather Coyote had come to him, surely. . . .

"And to you," the coyote said, with a little chuckle. That was the way of his kind, the chuckling laughter. There was only the tiniest trace of sarcasm in the chuckle this time. Or maybe the sarcasm was only in the mind of Red Horse, in his twinge of guilt.

"How goes your quest?" the spirit-guide asked, again with the hint of laughter.

"I . . . Uncle . . . I am not sure of my quest!" Red Horse blurted out.

He was confused. He was being questioned about his quest, and he did not even know what it was. The coyote chuckled again.

"Of course not! But you are seeking, that is good."

"But Uncle! What—?"

"It will come. . . ."

The figure of his spirit-guide was fading. He could see *through* the squatting form, see the sharp-pointed leaves of a yucca beyond, the shapes of pebbles on the sandy ground.

"Wait! Do not leave me, Uncle! I do not know. . . ."

But the spirit-guide was gone, and the plain was empty, except for a horse and rider. The horse drew a deep breath and expelled it in a sigh. Without any command, it started on.

At this point, the dream appeared to be over. Red Horse prepared to wake himself. *How strange, to prepare to awaken. One prepares to sleep, but . . .*

A distant drumming sound struck his ear, and he reined the horse to a stop to listen. The dream was not quite over. It was a familiar sound, a throbbing of the earth itself, the vibrating sound of life. The drumming of a thousand hoofs, or a thousand thousand, when the great herds run. Buffalo! Unconsciously, almost, he unslung his bow and drew an arrow from his quiver. He was in need of meat. . . . *How did he know that, in a dream?*

He saw the dust cloud before he could distinguish the running animals. They came from the south, a broad front looming out of the distance like the clouds of a summer storm. They swept closer, and the horse began to fidget nervously. It was a skilled buffalo runner and was impatient to begin.

Now Red Horse could make out individual animals in the running mass. In the space of a few heartbeats, the front line was upon him, and there was a moment of panic before the herd split to sweep past on either side. He began to seek a quarry. The horse spun to join the rush of the great herd, and a fat yearling swept abreast. Red Horse tugged his rein in that direction, and the skilled horse immediately sensed which animal was selected. They drew alongside the running buffalo, and he drew his arrow to the head and released it. The yearling stumbled and fell, and the herd swept on.

Red Horse managed to disengage his mount from the now-thinning herd and reined back to where the buffalo had fallen. He could not find it at first. He was disoriented by the clouds of dust that hung over the plain and made him cough.

As the dust began to settle, he saw the still, dark form and reined in that direction. It was a good, clean kill, the kind one dreams about, he thought with amusement. The feathered shaft projected not a hand's span beyond the flank, exactly where one wished to strike.

He dismounted now, and the horse stood, still breathing heavily. Red Horse walked over to the carcass and prepared to begin his task of butchering. But first, the apology. He tugged the head into a more lifelike posture and stood up to address it formally.

"My brother, I am sorry to take your life, but your flesh is my life, as the grass is yours. May your people prosper and be many—"

A sound from his horse, a snort of surprise . . . the young man whirled. There, only a few paces away, stood a magnificent buffalo bull. It was one of the largest he had ever seen, and it was pure white, white as driven snow! There was a moment to wonder how the white was not discolored from the dust that still hung over the plain. But such things can happen in dreams.

The creature was staring directly at him. He could clearly see the large red eye. It was so real . . . he should have felt fear, but there was none. Only awe. He had the feeling that the great bull was about to speak. Or, maybe, that *he* should.

"Good day to you, Uncle," he greeted.

The bull did not answer, but Red Horse could have sworn that the massive head nodded slightly. He thought he heard the chuckling laugh of a coyote. His spirit-guide, maybe, but more likely only a worldly coyote hoping to share his kill. He stood quite still, not moving, and the white bull did not move either. In the far distance, he could still hear the drumming of thousands of hooves, fading now.

Suddenly, the bull was gone, as if it had never been there. He whirled to look at his kill, and it too had disappeared without a trace. And his horse! . . . Panic gripped him, and he looked around quickly. In sight, there was nothing, only the flat, level plain, with the settling dust swirling along the ground like morning mists among the yuccas. He could still hear the distant drumming and, nearer at hand, the chuckling laugh. . . .

But he was waking now. The dusty plain and the yuccas were gone, and he lay in his sleeping robes in his own lodge. Through the smoke hole, he could see that the dark patch of sky was graying with the coming dawn. He half rose, sweating with the immensity of the things that he had seen.

The chuckle sounded again at his elbow. It was not the chuckle of his spirit-guide, or even of an earthly coyote, but the soft, throaty laugh of his wife as she snuggled against him.

"I am glad you are awake, Horse," she whispered. "You have been dreaming."

"Yes . . . yes, I have. Swallow, I . . . what is that sound?"

In the distance he could still hear the drumming that had been part of his dream. Could the buffalo—? No, not that, it was different.

Blue Swallow chuckled again. "I do not know," she told him. "It woke me, and I saw that you were dreaming. Maybe it is the drum of the owl prophet over in the camp of the Northern Band."

Red Horse nodded. "Maybe so," he said absently.

But he was thinking of a dusty plain far away, and of a magnificent white bull.

"Swallow," he said, "my dream . . . I must consider this. Maybe . . . maybe I can find the reason for the problems of the People."

"Are you sure?" she asked eagerly.

"I do not know. Let us say nothing, Swallow, until I think some more. And I must look again at the Story Skins and talk with my father."

Blue Swallow snuggled next to him but said nothing. She could tell when he was wrestling with things of the spirit.

4

>> >> >>

"What do you think this means, my son?" White Fox asked.

It had been barely daylight when Red Horse tapped on the lodge skin and poured forth his story. The two had studied the Story Skins and talked at great length. They had come to no clear conclusion. Finally South Wind had insisted that they eat something.

"Unless you are both beginning a fast today!" she chided.

Even that pause had hardly slowed their conversation.

"I do not know, Father," Red Horse said thoughtfully. "But I am made to think this is important."

"And I too. You had noticed the white buffalo cape in the Story Skins?"

"Yes . . . when all of us were looking, last night. Also the man's name, White Buffalo. You know of him?"

"Of course. He was a great holy man, many lifetimes ago. It was White Buffalo who learned and taught that the medicine of the buffalo and that of the elk-dog work well together. That led us to be called by some the Elk-dog People."

Red Horse nodded, still in awe of his dream.

"But this bull in your vision," White Fox pressed on. "It was a medicine animal?"

"So it seemed, Father. My spirit-guide told me to expect it."

"Ah!" exclaimed Fox. "That is important! But the white bull said nothing?"

"Nothing at all. It only stood there. I had made a kill for food, a good clean kill with an arrow—"

"Yes, so you said. This is remarkable detail for such a dream, my son. It *must* have meaning. Now, tell me again of this sandy plain."

Red Horse related again the details of his vision.

"Father," he said finally, "could this be the meaning? Are the People being told to go back to the importance of the two medicines, elk-dog and buffalo? I am made to think again of the loss of the white cape, here."

He pointed to the Story Skin, where the wearer of the cape was gored and tossed high in the air.

"Is this a sign?"

"Maybe," White Fox mused.

"Father, I am made to feel that there is something I should do."

"Hmm, yes . . . a new vision-quest, maybe?"

"Something like that. A search, a journey, or . . ."

They looked at each other as the realization dawned.

"A search for the white bull!" Red Horse whispered reverently.

"Of course!" White Fox was jubilant. "This will be the strength of the People's medicine! A return to the two medicines of White Buffalo!"

"Do you really think so, Father? This is a great responsibility! I am still learning, still searching for the gift of the spirit."

"And this is part of your search, my son. Who is better fitted? You are young and strong, and you are being *guided* in your search!"

"But, I—"

"I will cast the bones!" Fox said eagerly. "No, better . . . *you* cast them!"

He took down the little rawhide box and shook it gently. The sound was like that of a medicine rattle, the sound of small pebbles in the dried shell of the gourd-that-lives-forever. Fox handed the container to his son, while he spread the skin with geometric designs and carefully oriented it to the east, where the rising sun now shone through the door of the lodge.

Red Horse was nervous, his palms sweating. He had cast the bones before, but never for anything of this importance. Gently, he shook the container and, with a sweep of his arm, cast the contents across the skin. The dozen or so small articles rolled and skittered, dancing to a stop across the patterned surface: small pebbles of unusual shape or color, bits of carved bone or hard wooden fetishes, a couple of plum stones. The two men sat, studying the distribution of the objects.

White Fox began to point to various patterns, saying nothing but grunting with satisfaction.

"What do you think, Father?" asked Red Horse.

"No, my son! It is yours to interpret. You have cast the pattern."

Now his palms were really sweating. He wiped them on his leggings and cleared his throat.

"Well, first, the white stone."

It was a rounded pebble, a thing of great beauty, glistening pure white, and nearly round. He knew from experience that it could be expected to roll far. This time, however, it had seemed to have a life of its own. The white stone had nearly leaped off the edge of the skin.

"It finds its way far southwest," he noted.

White Fox nodded satisfaction.

"This is the direction of my quest."

His father nodded again.

Red Horse studied the fetishes, and the colors of the designs where they had stopped their skittering.

"The horse and the buffalo . . . they are nearly together, on the yellow. That is good. But there is danger." He pointed to some of the other objects. "Food and water . . . scarce. . . . Some enemies, maybe. But friends, too."

"Yes, it is good. A skillful reading, my son!"

There was emotion in White Fox's voice, as well as a degree of pride.

"When will you start?"

Red Horse thought for a moment. It was a big undertaking, perhaps the greatest of his life. He would need the best horse available, a supply of food, a waterskin.

"Maybe tomorrow."

"It is good," White Fox agreed.

Swallow took it well. At first she insisted that she would go with him, but he managed to dissuade her.

"I was alone, in my vision," he pointed out. "This is a quest that must be that way . . . like a vision-quest."

The truth of this interpretation was apparent.

"But I will help you prepare," she told him. "And we have tonight."

She said this with a mischievous smile that told more than words. It was a promise that she would make their last night together a memorable one. A night that would inspire him to hurry home when his quest was over.

But now there was much to do. A horse. He went to see about the possibilities while Swallow busied herself with packing some dried meat, spare moccasins, a robe.

"I have given this much thought," said White Fox, when asked about the horse. "There is such a horse, owned by our kinsman, Long Lance."

"But, Father, that is his prize buffalo runner. Lance would not let him go!"

White Fox smiled. "What use is a buffalo horse when there are no buffalo? We can ask."

The two approached the lodge of Long Lance. The lanky warrior was seated, leaning on his willow backrest.

"*Ah-koh,* brother," White Fox greeted him.

"*Ah-koh,* holy man."

The two seated themselves, and White Fox came directly to the point.

"Lance, we seek a mount for a special quest that Red Horse must take."

The leathery old warrior drew on his pipe, blew a cloud of fragrant smoke, and finally nodded.

"I have heard that he goes," he said.

The whole camp was aware, of course, but the exact nature of the mission was known only to the holy men and their wives.

"Let us go and look at the horses," Long Lance suggested.

He did not ask more details about the quest. Such questions would be impolite. It must be a mission of great importance, to leave just before the Sun Dance. The three men approached the grazing herd, and Lance called to one of the young men who tended the animals.

"Ho, Antelope! Bring the roan here!"

The youth waved in assent and threaded his way into the herd. Soon he returned at a trot, leading a magnificent stallion. The animal was not large, as horses go, but alert, well-formed, and athletic-looking. The large, well-spaced eyes were deep and knowing, showing knowledge and intelligence. His color was a uniform mixture of gray and red hairs, with black mane, tail, and stockings. Such a coat would appear different in different lights, constantly changing. This was Long Lance's favorite buffalo runner.

"But, Uncle," exclaimed the young man, "I could not take *this* horse!"

"What good is a buffalo runner when there are no buffalo?" Long Lance asked cryptically.

Red Horse wondered if the two older men had already talked of this and come to an agreement.

"But I cannot afford such a horse," he protested.

Long Lance peered at him, his face serious.

"My son, I know you would not come to me unless this quest is of great importance to the People. I do not know its purpose, but I know your heart and that of your father. You both have horses, but none is sufficient for this quest. So, if you seek my help, it is important. The horse is yours. Here, try him!"

Lance handed the lead rein to the young man. It had been a long speech for the usually quiet old warrior, and Red Horse was touched. He swung to the horse's back and reined around toward open prairie.

It was a strange mixture of feelings, to sit such a horse. Red Horse had never felt so much power under him, yet such easy control. He hardly had a need to guide the animal, for the roan seemed to know not only his slightest motion on the rein but also his slightest thought. The stallion was as quick as a cat, almost unseating the rider on one turn. But the feel of the rushing wind past his face, the confidence that the horse instilled . . . *aiee*, had there ever been such a horse?

"They work well together," observed Long Lance.

"Yes," answered Fox. "You have felt it too?"

Long Lance nodded. "Yes, I am made to feel that this is meant to be. I expected you this morning. A dream, maybe. It is important to the People, no?"

"Very important."

"Yes. Well, I must tell your son of this roan. This horse carries the blood of the First Elk-dog."

White Fox nodded. "I had heard that."

"But more! He is also of the blood of the Dream Horse, the great horse of the northwest!"

"*Aiee!* That I did not know. The one tamed by our ancestor Horse Seeker? I thought he freed the Dream Horse."

Long Lance laughed as he nodded. "That is true! He had promised, in return for the Dream Horse's help. But before Horse Seeker released the stallion, he bred all his mares!"

Both men chuckled.

"And this buffalo horse carries the blood of both!" White Fox marveled. "My brother, this is indeed the animal for the quest that Red Horse must take!"

"I am made to think so," said Long Lance seriously. "My brother, it is meant to be. Now, about the horse. He approaches the buffalo from the right—"

"Wait!" protested White Fox. "Tell these things to Red Horse. It is his quest."

"Of course," admitted Long Lance. "Come, let us sit and smoke, while he finds the spirit of the roan."

Long Lance led the way back toward his lodge.

"It would be good, would it not," he mused, "to be his age again and starting such a quest?"

The two men chuckled together, but then became serious.

"I am not certain," said White Fox, "that there has ever *been* such a quest."

Long Lance said nothing, for to question further about a medicine-quest would be very impolite, if not an outright taboo.

5
›› ›› ››

The horse was good, the best that Red Horse had ever ridden. It was a joy to try the different gaits, as he traveled toward the southwest that first morning. There was the smooth, swaying walk that brought comfort to the rider, like the comfort found by an infant in a cradleboard. The animal's trot, also, was not a jarring, bouncing thing, as in many horses. It too was a gait of fluid motion. The bounce that a trot requires at every step was cushioned and resilient, like that of the great hunting cat.

Probably the roan's most comfortable gait of all was an easy lope, in which every muscle seemed to flow in unison. It was a ground-eating pace. Red Horse would put the horse into the lope occasionally to ease the boredom for both mount and rider. After such an interval, when most horses would have been blowing heavily, the roan would still be breathing quite easily, hardly working up a sweat.

Once, just to experience it, Red Horse kicked the roan stallion into a hard run. The result was breathtaking. The animal flattened his little foxy ears to his skull and shot ahead like an arrow from a bow. The sprint was still smooth, but so fast . . . the wind roared past the ears of the young man, and he thought of the speed of a diving hawk as it drops to strike its quarry. He pulled the stallion in, resuming a trot and then a walk. The horse was blowing a little now. With amazement, Red Horse realized that in the excitement of the chase, the sprint would be even faster.

"Remember, he will approach from the right," Long Lance had told him as a parting bit of advice.

The dawn was just breaking when he had kissed Swallow good-bye and stepped up to mount the roan. His rawhide pack was tied carefully behind the saddle pad. His parents were there too, as well as Long Lance, to wish him a good journey.

"Yes, Uncle, it is good," he assured the old warrior. "I will use the bow."

The manner of the horse's approach was of great importance. Some horses preferred to approach the running quarry from the left. This was an advantage to a hunter who used the lance, because he strikes with the fixed lance held in his right hand and arm. A bowman, however, must hold the weapon in his left hand and draw the arrow with his right. Therefore, it was virtually impossible for a mounted bowman to shoot to his own right. He must have a horse that brought the target in range at the shooter's left.

The concern of Long Lance over his buffalo runner's style was understandable. He was a man who preferred the lance in the hunt, hence his name. And ordinarily, a horse with the approach from the right would be trained for a *bowman's* use. This was a spe-

cial circumstance, however. Long Lance, the renowned warrior and hunter, was left-handed. He
must have a horse that should have been chosen by a
bowman. Throughout his career, Long Lance had
trained his hunting horses very carefully, because of
this difference. He had become as respected for his
horses as for his skill as a hunter and warrior.

Now he nodded, assured that the young man understood the use of the roan stallion.

"May your trail be easy," he said.

There had been one other emotional moment as the
journey began. White Fox had approached his son just
before he mounted the roan. In his hand he carried
the elk-dog medicine, the Spanish bit that had been
worn by the First Elk-dog.

"Here, my son. Wear it and take strength from it."

Red Horse looked at the talisman, the emblem of
the People's first contact with the elk-dog. An animal
as big as an elk, so it had been described, but obviously
a dog because it carries burdens. It had been con-
trolled by this metal object in its mouth. That was long
ago, now. He looked at the bit, cleverly wrought of
iron, with the medicine ring circling the lower jaw of
the horse for firm control. The object was delicate yet
strong, beautifully wrought with decorative serpen-
tine curves. It was still further decorated with a series
of silver dangles, hanging from delicate links of silver
chain.

It was many lifetimes since the bit had actually been
placed in a horse's mouth. Generations of holy men
had worn it on a thong around the neck and had decorated it with strips of the finest fur of ermine and otter,
and with feathers of the eagle.

"No, Father. I could not wear this," Red Horse answered. "It might be lost. The elk-dog medicine is too important to the People."

"I am made to think," White Fox said simply, "that there is nothing more important to the People, just now, than your quest."

Fox had told the reassembled holy persons of the quest, though not about the white bull; only that Red Horse had been called by a vision. He had asked the others to use their respective medicines to petition for success in the quest. All had readily agreed to do so, though Cat Woman of the Eastern Band had of course expressed serious doubts.

Then White Fox had stepped forward and placed the thong of the elk-dog medicine around the neck of Red Horse.

"Wear it well, my son," he said.

Red Horse had been riding for most of the day. He had stopped briefly to talk with a hunting party of Head Splitters, who were having no luck in finding game. The two tribes were allies, and they rested their horses together at a sparkling stream while they discussed their common problem: Where had the buffalo gone?

"Is your Sun Dance over?" asked one man.

"No, it has not yet begun," Red Horse told them.

"*Aiee!* It is late, is it not?"

"Yes, things are not quite ready."

He felt a certain pride that would not let him tell how bad things really were. But he was sure they knew. The Head Splitters, while they had no Sun Dance of their own, had always been impressed by that of the People. They often attended, either by bands or as individuals.

"It is hoped," one said, "that your renewal ceremony helps bring back the herds."

Everyone nodded.

"How is it," another asked, "that you are leaving, just *before* your Sun Dance?"

"I have been called on a quest," Red Horse said vaguely.

"Oh."

There was nothing more to say. One did not ask details of another's quest, unless he volunteered information. And this Red Horse was not prepared to do. Conversation lagged, and one of the hunters rose from his squatting position.

"Come," he said to the others.

Then he turned to Red Horse.

"May your quest go well, my brother!"

"And your hunt," answered Horse.

He knew they recognized the seriousness of a quest that would take him away from the Sun Dance. Also, that such a quest might also be to their advantage.

"Aiee, I think our hunt is over." The Head Splitter chuckled ruefully. "Maybe we will move south this year and live on acorns!"

The others chuckled too, but with little mirth. The joke was too nearly true to hold much humor.

"At least there are bears there," Red Horse reminded. "We do not have that advantage!"

This brought a better laugh. It was one of the major differences between the two tribes. The People considered the killing of bears a religious taboo, while for the Head Splitters bear meat was a delicacy. For the People, this was next to cannibalism. There had always been a certain amount of good-natured banter about this difference.

"But there are deer and turkey there too," the

leader of the hunters offered. "Maybe we will see you in the oaks country."

"Maybe so," Red Horse admitted.

But he hoped for the success of his mission. He was not really sure what it was. He had seen a vision of the white bull, an important part of the People's heritage. He had an idea that the loss of the white cape long ago had somehow led to this present problem. But what was he supposed to do? If he found the bull and managed to kill it, then what? Must he tan the skin, fashion the cape and headdress? Then what?

Well, one thing at a time. First he must follow where the quest seemed to take him. One would not be called, he reasoned, without receiving further instruction when ready for it. He would wait.

He was sure that his direction was right. White Fox's bones had indicated that. Besides, had he not seen sand, rocks, yucca, and shortgrass in his vision? It would be many days of travel before he reached such country, but it was known to be to the southwest. He had talked with his father about the Southwest Trail, but they were agreed that it was not the area of his quest. The Southwest Trail led to Santa Fe and was familiar to the People, from when they traded there with the Spanish.

The area of Red Horse's quest must be south of there, they had decided.

"You will find it," White Fox had assured him. "One does not receive a call this strong, to be left wondering. You will be guided."

So he rode on. The country changed very little that first day. Red Horse became physically tired, but the thrill of excitement over his quest, the feel of the magnificent horse under him, kept him going. The gentle bump of the elk-dog medicine against the front of his shirt was reassuring.

Red Horse camped alone at a magnificent spring that gushed out of a hillside to form the headwaters of a stream. There was plenty of grass for the horse, and a clump of giant old oaks farther downstream. He built a small fire, not needed for warmth or for cooking but to establish his presence with whatever spirits might inhabit this place. He drank deeply but ate sparingly, to conserve his supplies. As he ate, he broke a small bit from one of his sticks of dried meat and tossed it into the fire, to appease any spirit that might be offended by his presence. This would help guarantee his success.

Finally, he lay down in his robe. He lay sleepless a long time, listening to the sounds of the night birds and the call of Kookooskoos, the hunting owl, in the timber below. He watched the Seven Hunters circle their way across the sky and fell asleep listening to the distant cry of coyotes on the ridge above. And it was good.

6

>> >> >>

Red Horse reined the stallion aside, but the animal jerked on the rein and turned back into the sandy creek bed. He pulled again, and the horse circled and tried again to take its own trail.

It was the first time the animal had misbehaved. Nearly a moon, they had traveled, and the roan stallion had performed perfectly all the way. They had lost weight, both of them. Red Horse was trying to conserve his slim food supply and did not mind the weight loss as a logical result. When he had the chance, he would eat and grow fat. Of course, there was no way of knowing when that might be. But he thought of the People, and his quest. He had come to believe that his was an awesome responsibility, a duty above and beyond the calling of the average holy man.

For the horse, he had more compassion. The animal lost flesh rapidly, and within ten sleeps it became apparent that some change was in order. He had been trying to cover as much distance as possible each day, to serve the purpose of his quest. It was tempting to push just a little farther, to use every bit of daylight each day. Especially so, with the comfortable gaits of the roan stallion. This provided more endurance for the rider, and the stamina of the horse seemed endless. So he had kept pushing a little harder.

He had realized his mistake almost by accident one evening, as he watched the graceful animal cropping grass just at dusk. Even in the poor light, the change was becoming apparent. The smoothly rounded curve of the hip, between hip bone and tail, appeared flatter. That was odd, thought Red Horse. The muscular, full shape of the hip and stifle had been one of the roan's most admirable features. He thought about it at some length and reached the inescapable conclusion. The horse was not getting enough to eat, to make up for the demanding punishment of long days of travel.

By a simple rule of thumb, the horse must spend half its time grazing to maintain weight and strength. This was not true of the buffalo. A herd could gorge rapidly on whatever vegetation offered and move on. Later, when opportunity offered, the buffalo could regurgitate and chew the hastily gulped forage, resulting in more efficient use. The horse, having no such method, must pick and choose better fare and chew it more thoroughly initially. Hence, it requires more time. *Aiee,* how could he have overlooked this? He must take better care of the animal.

This was not entirely out of compassion for the roan's welfare. If something happened to him, Red Horse, the roan stallion would survive quite well, left to its own devices. But, if the *horse* became disabled for any reason, the rider would be in a very dangerous situation. Water was becoming scarce. A man on foot might have slim chances of survival. There was less and less of the tallgrass prairie growth, here in the drier shortgrass country.

Well, he would do what he must: shorter days of travel, earlier camps. And he would consciously try to select the best areas for the roan to graze through the night. The short, curly buffalo grass was said to be excellent food for horses.

Even so, the roan gained back very little. It was a major effort just to prevent more loss. The country became drier, the grass more sparse, as they moved on southwest.

Now, it had been two days since they had found water. The fluid in his waterskin was gone, shared with the roan last evening. The country seemed strange, flat and sandy. There were no box canyons or gullies, at whose heads he might have searched for springs. At least, he could have in the Tallgrass Hills. He shifted the small, smooth stone on his tongue. That was said to make the mouth less dry. He had carried it there all morning and was beginning to doubt its effectiveness. But how would one know? Without the stone, he might be even more dry.

And now the roan was beginning to misbehave. He had not counted on this. He dismounted, quieted the stallion, and crooned reassuringly. Then he swung back up, only to have the horse begin to fight him again. Well, Red Horse decided, maybe the roan was aware of something that his rider did not know. Let him take the lead. He relaxed the rein, and instantly the roan turned to follow the dry stream bed.

Almost at once, Red Horse felt foolish. The horse would be better than he at finding water. The animal's sense of smell, its instinctive knowledge, would lead them. How could he have overlooked such a thing?

Well, the unfamiliarity of this semidesert country, he told himself. That was a thin excuse, and he felt little better. He should have thought of it.

Twice, the roan circled areas that appeared to offer perfectly solid footing. Red Horse knew that a horse senses places that are questionably dangerous to walk. These might be holes where the "sucking sand" could trap a horse and rider. Well, he would let the horse decide.

The roan pricked his ears forward and quickened his step, nostrils flaring. Ah, the animal's instinct had found water! But there was no water, only a dirty-looking smudge on the sandy creek bed, ringed by a cluster of yellow butterflies. The roan pushed forward, sniffing the damp spot in frustration. Red Horse's heart sank. Then the animal raised a forefoot and struck at the sand. The butterflies fluttered away, to return almost immediately. The hard hoof struck again, pawing at the darker area. Again, the butterflies scattered. A useless game. . . .

Suddenly, Red Horse realized the possibility. His brain must be baking in the sun, not to have realized before. They were in the area where the rivers run "upside down." The surface is dry, but beneath . . . he was already on his knees, digging with his hands, scooping sand to toss aside. The roan stood patiently.

In a short while, the young man had a pit a hand's span across and as deep. The sand that he was scooping was moist. He paused and watched a tiny puddle in the bottom of the hole grow and begin to fill. The horse nickered softly, nudging him impatiently.

"In a moment, my brother," Red Horse answered. "Yours is the first drink!"

He found a piece of thin, flat stone and used it to enlarge and deepen the hole. Three times he let it fill and allowed the horse to drink before the animal's thirst was satisfied. Then, as the roan wandered off to look for forage, he drank himself. Finally, his own thirst satisfied, he began to think more clearly.

It was early, but maybe it would be best to camp here for the night. Both he and the horse could satisfy their need for water, and the horse could forage in the brushy growth along the creek bank. He rose and gathered dry sticks among those same bushes. It was scant fuel, but the ritual fire was almost mandatory. He must notify the desert spirits of his presence here.

He lighted his fire and immediately felt better. Now it was a camp, a temporary home, and for tonight the center of his world. He began to think about food. *Aiee,* how he would like to smell roasting hump ribs of buffalo just now! It had been so long. . . .

There was a sudden snort from the roan, and he rose to investigate. Day was nearly gone, and . . . ah, yes! A rabbit. Carefully, he picked up his bow and fitted an arrow to the string. He slipped downstream toward the place where he had seen the long-ears, trying to keep low and stay at least partially hidden by the brushy growth. Yes, there! One of the lanky rabbits of the desert country. These were seen sometimes at home in the Sacred Hills, but cottontails were more commonly the quarry of the People—and then only in seasons of emergency, when buffalo and even dog meat was scarce. Some of the old women hunted rabbits with the throwing stick, as did children, learning to stalk game. . . . Well, this was an emergency.

He rose carefully and saw the rabbit, calmly sitting on its haunches, staring around. It seemed completely unconcerned, only mildly curious. Odd, he thought, that with such an attitude it had lived to grow up. One would have thought that some predator, a coyote or hawk, perhaps, would have seized it. He drew the arrow to its head and released it. The missile passed completely through the rabbit, bouncing across the sand beyond. The stricken animal ran, frantically trying to escape, even as it died, dragging itself more slowly in a wide circle until it collapsed, kicking its last.

Red Horse ran forward. He had had no fresh meat since his journey began. He picked up the rabbit and went to retrieve his arrow. Then, hungry as he was, he performed the apology.

"I am sorry to kill you, my brother. . . ."

Never was a formal apology more heartfelt, even for the finest, fattest buffalo cow ever taken in the hunt. He quickly skinned and gutted the animal and propped it on a stick near the fire. Then he turned to gather more fuel. This would be a good night: water and fresh meat. Sun Boy was painting himself in the western sky, to retreat to his lodge. The colors tonight were good. Flaming red, purples, and yellows.

The roan warned him. It was a nicker of greeting, by which a horse asks another, "Who are you?" Another horse? He whirled, trying to reach his weapon, but too late. Three well-armed warriors had materialized suddenly out of the brush. Their attitude said plainly that they considered him an intruder. Very carefully, he laid down his bow and raised a hand in the sign of peaceful greeting.

"Ah-koh, my brothers," he said.

A burly, bowlegged man who seemed to be their leader stepped forward. He did not bother to return the greeting sign.

"How are you called?" he demanded in hand signs. "What are you doing here?"

"I am called Red Horse," he signed carefully. "I am

of the Elk-dog People. I have water and a little meat.
Come, camp with me."

The bowlegged leader seemed unimpressed. "You
did not answer," he signed, "what you are doing here.
Now, is there any reason I should not kill you?"

He lifted his bow. Red Horse's palms were sweating,
but he knew he should show no fear, even though
panic gnawed at his stomach.

"Yes, my chief," he signed quickly, "but it requires a
little time to tell. You have wondered where the buffalo have gone?"

The three looked at each other, questioning. He
must be on the right trail.

"Come, sit," he urged. "I will tell you my story, and
then you can decide."

Boldly, he turned his back to lead the way to his fire.
He even stooped to pick up the sticks and the bow he
had dropped. He half expected an arrow between his
shoulder blades, but it did not come. Now, if he could
only keep their interest. . . .

7
>> >> >>

Red Horse walked over and renewed the fire, turning the broiling rabbit as he did so. Behind him, he could hear the padding footsteps of the strangers. It was all he could do to retain his composure and pretend that the situation was under control. He knew that at any moment one of these warriors might decide to kill him, on a whim, for his horse and weapons, even for the scrawny rabbit roasting at the fire. But he hoped that he had raised some interest, some questions in their minds, especially for the surly leader. He could not answer questions if he was dead, and it was to be hoped that the strangers would realize that fact.

He straightened and faced the three. They still appeared quite menacing.

"Now," he began, using hand signs, "maybe you have seen more buffalo than my people have."

It was obvious that they had not. Their garments and moccasins were well worn and patched. There was not a new-looking shirt, breechclout, or leggings among them, as there should have been after the spring hunts.

The men looked at each other and back to him, ready to listen now. They realized that he could see their situation.

"My moccasins are thin too," he signed. "Where are the buffalo?"

He did not expect an answer. His question was purely for effect. He was gaining confidence.

"Look," he continued, "we have the same problem. Maybe we can help each other."

The bowlegged one chuckled, but it was without humor.

"We do *not* have the same problem," he signed, using short, choppy gestures. "*We* do not hunt in someone else's hunting ground!"

"*Aiee!* The rabbit? That is only while passing through. I have offered to share it, as you would in my country!"

There were nods of agreement, though the surly leader remained unconvinced.

"You spoke of reasons I should not kill you," that one recalled, "but I have seen none."

"Because we seek the same thing, Uncle. To bring back the buffalo. I can help your people do that."

Such a statement stretched truth a little, and the warriors realized it.

"How?" one signed.

"My medicine is strong," he indicated. "I am on a vision-quest, a special quest for the buffalo."

"What is that to us?" demanded Bow-Legs.

But his attitude was changing. There was great respect for another's medicine, even that of an enemy. And in this case, the stranger's goal would benefit all.

"If I bring back the buffalo," Red Horse signed, "it helps your people *and* mine."

"True." The other nodded. "What is your medicine? This?"

He pointed to the dangling bit around Red Horse's neck.

"Partly," Red Horse indicated. "This is the elk-dog medicine of my people. Mine is also the medicine of the buffalo."

"You are a holy man?" one of the others asked.

"Yes. I have a vision that sends me on this quest."

"This elk-dog medicine," persisted Bow-Legs. "I have heard of its strength and power. Why should I not take it from you?"

Red Horse tried not to show his fear. Near panic, actually. He reached back into his memory to recall something that might be of use. Playing for time, he managed a chuckle.

"My chief," he signed, "surely a leader such as yourself is well aware of the dangers of interfering with another's medicine." He paused for a moment, and then continued as he saw the desired look appear on their faces. "Long ago, this medicine *was* stolen by an enemy. He wore it as I do, but he was killed by it."

There was a gasp from the youngest of the warriors.

"How?"

"Strangled. By this very thong," Red Horse gestured dramatically.

It was quite true. Horse Seeker, it was said in the legends of the People, had killed a huge enemy chief, Walks-Like-Thunder, by twisting the thong with a broken lance shaft.

"But come," Red Horse invited. "Let us drink, eat, and smoke, and talk of our search for the buffalo. There is water there."

He had succeeded, at least for the present. The three sauntered over and drank from his dry-river well, one or another always keeping an eye on Red Horse as he tended the fire. The rabbit was browning nicely now, and the smell of fresh meat mixed with the smoke of the fire. Finally, Red Horse lifted the stick and displayed the browned rabbit.

"It is not buffalo," he signed in apology, "and not much, but better than hunger."

This produced an appreciative chuckle from the others. The sign for hunger, a cutting motion across the abdomen, suggested a literal meaning: "Better than a knife in the stomach." Red Horse was working hard at injecting humor. It is hard to kill a man who makes you laugh.

It is also hard to kill someone with whom you have shared meat. Red Horse carved off the left hindquarter and handed it to the bowlegged leader. This was regarded as the choice portion, and to offer it first represented honor to the leader of these strangers. Bow-Legs only grunted and began to eat, while Horse divided the rest among the others.

The meal was quickly over and the bones sucked clean. One rabbit does not go far among four hungry travelers. It was growing dark now, and one of the younger warriors went to bring their horses to water. He returned with an armful of dry fuel, and Red Horse renewed the fire.

"Let us smoke and talk," he suggested, after these necessary chores were finished. "I have tobacco."

He passed the pouch, and the others filled pipes. This would be a social smoke, not the formal medicine-pipe ceremony. Bow-Legs took a stick from the fire to light his pipe and blew a fragrant cloud.

"It is good," he admitted grudgingly. "What do you use?"

"My people mix a leaf called sumac with the tobacco," Red Horse explained. "It is a plant that grows to the east of here."

"I have heard of it." The chief nodded. "Red willow, shaved and toasted, is good too."

"I like cedar bark," one of the others noted. "Or, sometimes, a few cedar leaves."

"That burns hot, though," the third man protested.

"Not unless it is too dry."

They were using hand signs for the benefit of Red Horse, as well as talking aloud among themselves. An idea struck him. The range of this tribe must adjoin that of the Head Splitters.

"Do you speak the tongue of the Head Splitters?" he asked in signs.

"A little," answered Bow-Legs suspiciously. "Do you know them?"

Red Horse was afraid that he had made a mistake. Suppose these were bitter enemies of the Head Splitters?

"A little," Red Horse signed casually. "Their country meets ours on the south and west. We see them sometimes."

"We, too. Sometimes we even trade a little."

"Then we both know some of their tongue," suggested Red Horse.

Bow-Legs nodded. This would make conversation somewhat easier, a combination of hand signs and a spoken language known to some degree by all those present.

"Let us talk, then," Bow-Legs said. "Tell us what you are doing here."

Red Horse described his vision in some detail and

told of the discussion and planning with his father, the senior holy man.

"I am made to think," he finished, "that a part of the problem for my people is a forgetting of the old ways. There was a talisman, a fetish, that was lost long ago. Maybe I can restore it and bring back the buffalo."

He did not feel it necessary to tell of the white bull, and the others did not ask. They were nodding in understanding. Then one of the younger warriors spoke.

"I am called Owl-in-the-Ground," he began, "or Digging Owl. I too am a holy man. That is why *we* are here."

"To find the buffalo?" asked Red Horse, astonished at the holy man's revelation.

The other nodded. "In our legends, the herds came out of a hole in the ground."

"Yes, it is the same with us," Red Horse said eagerly.

"So maybe they went back." Digging Owl shrugged.

Red Horse had not thought of that interpretation. But Digging Owl was continuing.

"Maybe they go down that hole every winter, and someone has plugged the hole."

Red Horse nodded tentatively. If one could accept the Creation story of the plains tribes, why not the suggestion of this holy man?

"If we can find the hole and reopen it, the buffalo will return," Owl continued.

Red Horse was not certain that he was ready to accept this whole theory, but one thing was plain. Their goals were one.

"Maybe," he said cautiously. "I saw buffalo in my vision, but no hole."

"And I a hole, but no buffalo!" stated Digging Owl. "Maybe we have two parts of the same vision."

"Maybe. Whether it is so or not, we seek the same thing."

There was a long silence, broken by Digging Owl. "Maybe it is meant that we should travel together."

Red Horse, too, was slow in answering. "Which way are you going?" he asked.

"We have traveled southeast," Owl said. "This was in my vision."

"And southwest in mine," answered Red Horse. "Our trails cross?"

"That seems unlikely. Maybe we are both meant to turn south now."

"But how will we know?" Red Horse wondered.

"Let us sleep on it," suggested Digging Owl. "We will talk again in the morning. I will go west a little to sleep, you go east, and we will listen for our spirit-guides."

It was a good plan. The two holy men took their robes and prepared to move some distance in their respective directions. The other two men stayed by the fire.

"I am made to think we should each have a fire," Red Horse suggested. "That will announce our presence to whatever spirits may be looking for us."

"It is good," Owl agreed.

Each took a burning stick from the fire, and they parted.

Red Horse sat on his robe a long time, watching the stars rotate overhead. He could see the main campfire off to his right and, farther yet, the fire of the other holy man. From time to time a shower of sparks fluttered into the sky, indicating that Owl had tossed more sticks on his blaze.

In the distance, coyotes called, and he thought of his spirit-guide. He hoped he would be able to sleep, to be receptive for whatever his guide might choose to reveal. He was looking south, the direction in question, when a falling star streaked across the blackness of the sky, like an arrow arching its way. And its way was south. Just as it happened, a long, chortling coyote call sounded from the same direction. Red Horse smiled to himself.

"Thank you, Grandfather," he murmured, half aloud.

Without another thought, he rolled in his robe and fell asleep. There were no dreams or night-visions. None were needed now. The trail had been marked.

"**D**id you see it?" asked Digging Owl.

It was barely daylight when they came together at the central campfire.

"The falling star? Yes."

"It pointed south."

"Yes. It is good," Red Horse observed.

"You are going together?" asked Bow-Legs.

"Yes, Uncle," Red Horse answered. "We have been given the same sign."

The surly chief nodded. "Maybe it is good that we did not kill you." He looked from Owl to Horse and back again. "Will your two medicines work together?"

Digging Owl answered for both. "We are made to think so, Uncle."

"Then go, and may your trail be easy."

"But—you are not coming too?" Red Horse asked, startled.

"There is no need now. Your medicine and that of

Owl, here, will work or not. If it does, we get the buffalo back. If not, you die, and our nations are no better off, but no worse either. So, it is good. Lame Wolf and I are going home."

In a remarkably short time, those two had saddled their horses and were gone. Red Horse and Digging Owl looked at each other. This was happening too fast.

"Do you know this country?" asked Red Horse. "It is outside the range of my people."

"Mine too. But we know it some."

"Then you lead. Is there water? That was my worry."

"And right, to worry. But there are streams . . . upside down, at this season," Owl said.

"Yes. My horse showed me. And game?"

"Rabbits. A few antelope. Real-snakes."

"*Aiee!* Your people eat real-snakes?"

"No, but sometimes one eats what he must."

To himself, Red Horse fervently wished that this quest would not lead to the eating of real-snakes. The two broke camp and rode out, with Digging Owl leading the way. Owl was good at this semidesert existence, Red Horse decided. Distant landmarks, the way the People established direction, were almost nonexistent here.

It took most of the morning for him to discern how Digging Owl maintained his course. Each yucca, each clump of coarse grass, and each of the grassy bushes that managed to eke out an existence here cast a shadow. When they started to travel, looking south with the rising sun in the east, the shadows pointed straight west. As the morning passed, the shadows became shorter and shorter and finally almost disappeared. Red Horse was looking in vain for a landmark to the south, but the country was flat. There was no hill or rock or even a tree that would have a distinctive enough appearance to use for establishing a course. He was about to mention it when Digging Owl abruptly called a halt.

"We rest," he indicated, turning his horse loose to forage among the sparse growth. He took a straight length of yucca stalk and stuck it upright in the sand. There was hardly any shadow.

Of course, Red Horse thought. When Sun Boy's torch was directly overhead, this manner of telling direction was almost useless. The only thing to do was to wait. Owl spread his robe for a place to sit, and Red Horse did likewise.

"Tell me of your people," Digging Owl requested.

It was the customary form of entertainment when different tribes camped together. This exchange had been neglected the night before, in the urgency of their chance meeting. Now, with more leisure, these two would share their people's traditions, beliefs, and legends. It had become apparent last night that Digging Owl understood the language of the Head Splitters quite well.

"It is good," said Horse in beginning. "I will use the Head Splitters' tongue?"

Owl nodded, smiling. "I was uneasy last night. Maybe you were their enemy."

"Yes." Red Horse laughed. "I thought so of you, too."

Now that they had a basis of understanding, the two could use this language known to both, though native to neither.

"My people," Red Horse began, "came into the world from inside. They lived in darkness, but crawled out into the sunlight through a hollow cottonwood log. The Old Man—Man of the Shadows—sat on the log

and tapped it with a drumstick. Out came First Man
and First Woman, then others."

He paused and waited. This was a part of the story,
an inside joke. No one could resist the pause for long,
and usually asked the same question.

"Are they still coming out?" asked Owl.

"No," said Red Horse sadly. "A fat woman got stuck
in the log, and no more could come through. This is
why our nation has always been small!"

Both laughed.

"But your people are well respected," Owl observed. "You had the first horses. How was that?"

"I am not sure," Red Horse admitted. "Others had
horses too, but more to the south and west. Your people, probably, very early. We were some of the first on
the plains. An outsider, called Heads Off, a warrior
with fur on his face, brought the First Elk-dog. We are
called Elk-dog People on the plains, because of this.
But the Head Splitters, who were our enemies then,
had elk-dogs too."

"Yes. We too. The Spanish had them in Santa Fe."

"Yes. Did you know we traded in Santa Fe, until the
war?"

"Ah! You were far from home!"

"Yes. My father, White Fox, was there when the war
came. The Spanish put him in a cage."

"You know they are back now?"

"The Spanish? Yes, we heard that. But we have not
gone back to trading there."

Digging Owl was an interesting companion. The
two were of similar age. Owl had a wife and a small
daughter, while Red Horse and Swallow had no child
yet. The noon halt passed rapidly, and it seemed all
too soon that Owl stood and shook out his robe to
continue travel. Yes, Red Horse could see a small but

growing shadow on one side of the stick now. That would be east. They moved on, to the south.

It was late in the afternoon when they encountered a wide, dry stream bed.

"Maybe we should camp here," Digging Owl suggested. "There should be water."

They rode up and down the stream bed for some time before Owl selected a spot. Red Horse was pleased that his roan stallion seemed to have selected the same place. They were forced to dig somewhat deeper here, and Red Horse had a few moments that approached panic before he saw the first handfuls of damp sand emerge from the hole. This was not a country he would choose, he reflected. It was good that some had different preferences.

It was a beautiful evening, however, cooling rapidly after Sun Boy sought his lodge. Digging Owl insisted that they camp some distance from the stream bed, and on the side that was slightly higher, to avoid the danger of a flood. Red Horse was amused, for a moment, but then remembered his own country. Rains far upstream could sometimes cause a flash flood to come crashing down into valleys where no rain had fallen. It could be a dangerous situation, and he would do well to listen to Digging Owl, who was experienced in this strange land where the rivers ran upside down.

There was one other advantage to the location of their camp. Just before dark a lone antelope, apparently scenting their water from far off, stepped daintily along the sandy stream and paused to look around. Digging Owl dropped the creature with a well-placed arrow.

Red Horse was pleased to note Owl's apology, which seemed much like his own would have been, though in another tongue. The signs were good for the success of a mission such as theirs. As the two dined on fresh meat, they decided to camp for a day to dry some of the meat for the journey. They did not know how long their trail might be, or how lean the hunting.

They ate, then butchered out the best cuts of meat for their purpose and placed it near their campfire. It was not long before a pair of coyotes, who had probably scented the kill some time before, came to share the bounty that had been left in the stream bed. They could be plainly seen by the light of the rising moon.

"Eat well, my brothers." Red Horse spoke quietly.

The two sought their robes, and Horse lay awake a long time, thinking about all the new twists to this quest, especially of Digging Owl, the holy man from an unfamiliar tribe. After the initial danger in that unexpected meeting, things had appeared to progress quite well. All the signs had been good: the falling star; the presence of the coyotes, which seemed to imply that his spirit-guide was near; the unlikely alliance with a stranger, also a holy man, whose quest seemed the same.

Even the young man's name had something familiar about it. Digging Owl . . . wait! The Story Skins! The legend represented there, about the loss of the white buffalo cape! There had been two medicine men, one killed by a buffalo—apparently the evil one. The one who survived appeared in later pictographs in favorable situations. And that holy man's name had been . . . *Owl!* Yes, he clearly remembered the pictures in the circles: an owl's head. It had appeared to be the likeness of Kookooskoos, the horned hunting owl, of course. Kookooskoos was probably not known here in the desert country. The owls here lived in holes in the ground, like prairie dogs, hence the name of the young holy man who was now his companion.

The digging owl. How strange. Was there a sign here of some sort? Was it only coincidence that a renowned holy man of his own nation had the same name as this holy man who now shared his quest? Both were concerned with the white buffalo cape: one with its loss, the other with its recovery.

And what *was* the purpose of Digging Owl's quest? The man had been rather vague about what his quest involved. But so had Red Horse himself. He had told Owl nothing about the white cape. Did Owl know of the cape? Was it possible, even, that the legends of both nations were similar, that their stories were the same, that the time might come when he and Digging Owl would have to compete for the white cape?

He found this a disturbing thought, but he was tired from a day's travel in the hot sun and comfortably full in his belly. Tomorrow would be a long day, preparing and drying meat. He must rest, but sleep was slow in coming.

Finally he fell asleep with the nagging question still unresolved. Were the quests of the two holy men so similar that they would be pitted *against* each other when the time came?

9

>> >> >>

Red Horse watched the other man closely as they rode. It was not a matter of enmity, or even suspicion. The two had enjoyed each other's company. Maybe it was only that their cultures were so different, he thought. Digging Owl could probably not understand anyone who lived in tallgrass country, any more than he, Red Horse, could understand people who made the desert their home.

They had shared and enjoyed their Creation stories, and other legends of their two nations. They had shared meat and had drunk from the same sand springs. Surely, their spirits should be as one. But there was a reluctance, a hesitancy, a lack of . . . well, a lack of complete trust. And it was uncomfortable. This was not the way of his parents, or the way he had been raised. Why? He asked himself. Why was there this barrier between him and Digging Owl? Why were they able to talk endlessly about something

as remote as Creation, to delight in each other's stories, yet talk very little about their quest together for
the buffalo? Neither had made any definite statements
at all, in the several sleeps they had traveled and
camped together. What would they do, together or
individually, when they found the herds, or the hole in
the earth, or whatever they might find?

Red Horse tried to tell himself that it was because
they did not know what lay at the end of the trail. But
did he not know? The white bull. His vision had suggested the white bull as the end of his quest. He had
not shared that with his companion. Why not? he
asked himself, but could not answer. It was a private,
personal thing, like discussing one's medicine. It was
simply not done.

Yet if he had refrained from telling Owl of his entire
purpose on the quest, was it not likely that Owl, too,
had held something back? That was to be expected. It
was as reasonable for Digging Owl to do so as for
Horse. Why should he be suspicious? Still, he had the
strong feeling that Owl was suspicious too.

The distrust was hanging more heavily between
them each day. They talked, but of the trail and their
campsites. Sometimes of their tribal stories, which
they still found pleasure in sharing. But increasingly
they were avoiding any talk of their quest, their reason for being together. They could talk of anything
but that. Though the signs were good, and continued
so, the hesitancy remained.

Red Horse watched a hawk circling on fixed wings
high above. It was hunting, no doubt, able to see its
quarry for as far as a day's travel. He wondered what it
might be like, to hang far above the earth. . . . *Aiee,*
he had forgotten. In his dream, he had done so. He had

watched himself ride across the plain. But . . . he had been alone, had he not?

His thoughts were interrupted by the hawk's cry. Three times, the bird screamed the long-drawn, high-pitched scream of its kind. Then, as it completed another circle against the bright blue, it shot away to the south. Its wings were still fixed, but its speed increased as the creature moved like an arrow. Straight and swift, it traveled on an invisible current, as nearly due south as a mere mortal could discern.

"It is good!" said Digging Owl at his elbow.

"Yes." Horse answered.

Why could they not discuss this further?

"The signs are still good," Horse ventured.

"Yes," agreed Digging Owl.

They fell back into the embarrassed silence.

That night over the fire, they attempted to talk. Both were feeling the problem, Red Horse believed. Their meeting had been unusual from the start, with the strong possibility of violence. It had been such a relief to learn that they were really on the same mission, that both were holy men, and that they were receiving the same signs. When the two warriors left them, it had been like the lifting of a great trouble. They, these two, could understand each other and could learn from each other's knowledge. It had seemed good, but the situation had fallen apart from that point.

They had shared stories with great enjoyment, but after the first day there had grown this widening gap between them. By now, they were hardly speaking. This in spite of the fact that both continued to read the signs alike, and they continued to be favorable.

Digging Owl brought up the subject at the fire that night.

"My friend," he began hesitantly, "there is something wrong here. Do you feel it?"

Red Horse nodded. "Of course. But what is it?"

"I cannot tell." Owl pondered. "But our signs are still good."

"Yes. That is most puzzling."

Red Horse finished the strip of dried meat that he was chewing and drew out his tobacco pouch. He packed his short pipe and then handed the pouch to Owl.

"Have you shared a quest before, with other holy men?" Owl asked.

"Only with my father. He is the eldest of my nation. . . . Well, before my vision, he had called together all the holy men. Two are women, however."

"Ah! Women?"

"Yes. Some of our women have the gift. One from her husband, who passed it on to her. She was his assistant. Then there is one who is an herb healer."

"That is very interesting," observed Digging Owl. "But go on. There was this meeting?"

"Yes. My father asked everyone to pray and seek visions on the same night."

"But only you had one?"

"I do not know. Others did not say. There was one, an owl prophet from one of the other bands, who beat his drum all night. Do you think his medicine is like yours?"

Owl shrugged. "Who knows? No one's gift is exactly like another's. But what of the others? You had no problems explaining your vision?"

"No . . . well, Cat Woman—the herb doctor—always says no to everything."

Both men chuckled, and Horse went on.

"No, but of course I did not tell them all of my vision."

About the white bull, he was thinking. *And I did not tell you either, my friend. Some visions are not meant to be shared.*

"Of course," Digging Owl was saying, "just as we did not tell each other everything."

Red Horse was startled, uneasy. He was not quite ready to discuss that. Not openly, at least. He decided to change the subject slightly.

"Owl," he said, "you know this country better than I. Is its spirit one that comes between us?"

"Maybe," said Owl thoughtfully. "I do not know. This is not really my people's country, you know."

"Yes, but it is more like yours than mine."

"That is true. But what of its spirit?"

It was well known that the spirit of a place affects the lives of people. Red Horse had been in spots that were brooding, forbidding, that made him want to run, to escape. There were places known to the People where bad, evil things had happened, to such an extent that these areas were avoided. By contrast, there were favorite places, whose spirits were good and comfortable and inspiring. But this place?

"I do not know," Red Horse said. "I feel . . . maybe I am not in touch with its spirit."

Owl nodded. "It is not an easy spirit to know," admitted Owl. "But you do not feel it as evil?"

"No, no. Do we not have good signs here, both of us?"

"Yes, that is what I mean. Then why do we not trust each other?"

Horse shook his head, puzzled. "That is what I have

wondered. Is it because we are both uneasy, in a strange country?"

"Maybe. But Horse, is it because we do not trust each other's *medicine?*"

Red Horse considered that for a little while. One questions that which is unfamiliar.

"Can it be that our medicines conflict with each other?" he asked.

He was still worrying about Owl's quest. Specifically, had Owl's vision sent him also to seek and kill the white bull, for *his* nation's medicine?

"I have wondered too," Owl said slowly. "But our goal is the same, to bring back the buffalo."

"And our signs are the same," Horse added. "Do we only question because we do not know each other? Each other's medicine? Our nations are very different."

"As they should be. But we cannot share our gifts . . . you do not share yours, even among your own holy men. Tell me, Horse, do you tell your holy man father *all* of your visions?"

"Usually. We talk of them."

"But not always."

Horse was beginning to see the other's way of thinking. It was not each other they distrusted, but the power of each other's medicine. Horse had felt from the start that the medicine gift of Digging Owl was very powerful and to be respected. No doubt Owl had felt the same about his. When one comes in contact with an unfamiliar power, he is uneasy.

"I see what you are saying," he agreed. "We do not know the powers of each other."

"But we do not need to know, if their purpose is the same," Owl pointed out. "And it must be. Our signs say so."

Of course! Both had made the same error, that of trying to understand each other's medicine, instead of merely welcoming the help. Red Horse laughed.

"If it is any comfort," he volunteered, "my medicine gift cannot be used to hurt."

"And mine!" Owl answered. "If I used it to kill you, it would kill me also."

"Let us not talk of killing. We sound like your bow-legged chief."

Digging Owl laughed. "Yes, that is his answer to most things. But I am made to think we need each other."

"I too. And, about the danger of misusing your gift . . . mine is the same. It would kill me."

Owl smiled. "I suspected that."

"Then we do not need to know each other's gifts, to benefit from both?" Horse asked.

"I think not. Only to be ready to experience them."

Both men slept better that night, now that they shared a better understanding. Red Horse even dreamed of his spirit-guide. The coyote stalked past at a little distance, turning only to chuckle in good-natured derision at the effort that two holy men had expended merely to agree. He did not speak.

"Thank you, Uncle," Red Horse called to him.

The only answer was another amused chuckle. Or maybe that was merely the laughing call of the real-world coyotes, talking to the rising moon.

10
⟩⟩ ⟩⟩ ⟩⟩

The old woman sat and smoked and watched the distant riders. She had seen them and watched them for most of the day, as they crossed the dry plain toward her.

At first she was not certain. They could have been a couple of stray buffalo, though she had seen none since the great herd passed, last season. That was odd. The buffalo should have reappeared, on their way back north, when the world began to warm again. She had wondered greatly about it and had prayed and performed her chants. But no buffalo had returned.

Where had they gone? Had the seasons changed, somehow? The weather had been different, unpredictable, for the past season, but the great migrating herds had to be somewhere. They could not simply vanish from the earth, or into it. Or could they? Anything was possible, she had decided long ago. Her own life was proof of that.

She had been only twelve summers old when she was stolen and carried away, to be raised in a culture quite foreign to her own. She would probably not have survived, if it had not been for the early teachings of her grandmother, who was a respected medicine woman.

"You are special, my child," the old woman had explained. "You have the gift. I knew, soon after you were born, by the wise look in your eyes."

New Grass had been excited, could feel her heart thump and her palms become damp.

"What must I do, Grandmother?" she asked.

"Nothing for now, little one, only learn all you can. The important thing is that you *know* of your gift. Cherish it, learn, and prepare to use it when the time comes."

"And when is that?" the child had asked excitedly.

The old woman had chuckled to herself. "It will be many winters, child. After you have grown, taken a husband, and raised a family of your own."

"Aiee, that long? Why do we speak of it now, Grandmother?"

"So that you do not *lose* the gift. If you forget, it would appear that you are refusing the gift, and it might be taken from you."

"I see. Why must I wait?"

"Because of the taboo. A holy woman must be past the age of menstruation. Then she begins to use the gift."

"Did you do so, Grandmother?"

"Of course. I was told, as I am telling you, by a holy woman who taught me."

"Does my mother have this gift?"

The grandmother chuckled again. "I am not sure. Sometimes I have thought so. She may have to wait to find it until she no longer needs to go to the menstrual lodge. That happens, sometimes. But her medicine— her gift—is not like yours. Now come, I will teach you of plants and herbs. You can learn that part now."

New Grass had been only six or seven then. She learned hungrily, using what she was permitted, storing the rest in her memory. Her relationship with her grandmother had been a wonderful thing. They laughed together and shared little secrets. Sometimes Grass could tell what her grandmother was thinking, and it was good.

It was a summer or two later that New Grass found out she could sometimes see into the future. That was a frightening thing. She had shared the discovery with her grandmother, of course.

"I saw a dream. Broken Lodge Pole was killed in the hunt, Grandmother."

"Tell me more, child." The old woman's brow had been furrowed with concern.

"That is all. I saw him tossed high by a bull, and he died."

Grandmother clucked her tongue in dismay. "Let us say nothing of this to anyone, child. Not for now. We will speak of it again."

Only three sleeps later it had happened. New Grass was playing with her doll when she heard the plaintive wail of the Song of Mourning come drifting through the camp. The men were out hunting. She jumped and ran to find Grandmother, but fear clutched at her heart.

"Grandmother! Is it—?"

"Hush, child, let us wait and see."

They stood together, and it was not long. Black Dog rode past, slumping dejectedly on his horse.

"Ho, there, Dog!" Grandmother called. "What is it?"

Black Dog reined in for a moment. "The herd turned the wrong way," he explained. "Lodge Pole is dead."

"*Aiee!* How?"

But New Grass knew already.

"A great bull. He was tossed high and came down among the buffalo," Black Dog said as he reined away.

Grass was frightened. "Grandmother! It is as I saw it! What must I do?"

"I was afraid of this," Grandmother said softly. "This is a gift of mixed blessings that you have, child. It may be more of a curse. You will have to decide, each time this happens, whether to tell anyone."

"But how? How can I decide, Grandmother?"

"That is the curse, child. Sometimes it may be kinder to say nothing. Other times, maybe you can help by warning someone."

"But that is too hard. Do *you* have this gift, Grandmother?"

"No, child. The gifts of each are different. But you must remember yours and follow as you see fit. You can refuse the gifts if you like."

"No, I will not refuse," the girl mused. "But the load is heavy, Grandmother."

"Yes, my child. I do not envy you this gift."

The odd thing, perhaps, was that the gift, or curse, of foresight was unpredictable. Sometimes it was present, sometimes not. Sometimes it was there for completely inconsequential things, like a misplaced awl, but not for a major tragedy such as a death in the village. The girl always shared these premonitions with her grandmother, who continued to caution her to secrecy.

"If no one knows you have this gift, you cannot be blamed for warning them or not."

New Grass could see the wisdom of this, though it was sometimes difficult to say nothing.

"Suppose your gift is known," Grandmother said. "Then anyone who has bad luck will be angry that you did not warn him."

"But maybe I did not *see* his bad luck!" Grass protested.

"That is the point! If your gift is known, you will be blamed anyway."

So she had kept it a secret. It had not helped her any when the time had come for Grandmother's crossing over. Grass had no warning at all. One day, the grandmother had seemed perfectly healthy, and the next she was gone. It had been a time of great loss for the girl. She felt abandoned, alone. No one else in all the world could understand this loss.

It was while she was a distance outside the camp, engaged in private mourning, that she had been abducted.

She tried to be a cooperative prisoner, to achieve better treatment, yet she resolved to escape. But she was carried far away, and with winter coming, her escape was postponed. Maybe in the spring?

By that time, however, she had been traded to another captor, and lost to still another in a gambling game played with sticks. When menstruation announced her arrival at womanhood, her value increased, and she was traded again.

Finally, now far from home, she did manage to escape and was taken in by a gentle people who lived in lodges made of mud bricks. There was a young man who was kind to her, and it became easier to respond to his advances than to consider going alone to search for her own people. That idea never really left her mind, of course. It was merely postponed once again, first for the winter, then for the courtship that resulted in marriage.

She told her husband of her gifts, and of her intention to become a medicine woman after their children were grown. The young man was horrified.

"You cannot do this!" he told her harshly. "Such things are not for women!"

"Among my people—" she began, but he stopped her short.

"You are not among your people!"

She was hurt, but it was useless to argue. She continued to learn all she could of this strange dry country and to welcome, rather than deny, her gifts of the spirit. But she told no one. When the time was right, she would go home.

They had two children, who were bright and loving, and she was a good mother and an obedient wife, always looking ahead.

The children were grown and in their own lodges when her premonition startled her with a warning about her husband. In the dream, she saw a great fat lizard, the dreaded kind with skin like a beaded yellow-and-black medicine bag. She saw it bite him, and she awoke with a cold sweat, crying, and he held her close. She sobbed out her story, but he only laughed. He could not be convinced.

She had already started to pack some supplies for traveling when they came to tell her that he was dead, killed by the poisonous bite of the lizard.

"I know," she said.

After the burial and the prescribed period of mourning, she announced to her children that she was going home. They attempted to dissuade her, as did her husband's family, but it was no use. Now, at long last, she could seek her life's goal, return to her own people.

It was several sleeps to the northeast of the pueblo that had been her home that the realization came to her. She had camped on a little knoll overlooking flat prairie in all directions, and she was enthralled by the distance that she could see. As the moon rose, silvering the world with beauty, she realized she could no longer go home. It would not be the same. The people she had known as a child were either dead or changed, as she was herself—so much, probably, that she would not know them. And, though her early years had been spent in the culture of her people, most of her life had been spent in learning the ways of the desert and the pueblos. That had become her life.

There was an increasing suspicion, also, that this new phase, like her abduction, was part of a pattern. She became convinced it was time to assume her responsibilities as a holy woman, and that assumption proved true. After the death of her husband, she never menstruated again.

She had stayed awake all night on her rocky knoll, spending much time in prayer. By morning she had reached a decision. She would stay right there. She was caught between two worlds, two cultures. So was this spot. To the west and south lay the desert, and to the east the dry shortgrass country. She could see the change before her. How appropriate, and how peaceful, this existence!

The next morning she circled the area, seeking to verify her impression of the night. Yes, there was a stream, and a level area where she might grow corn and pumpkins for her use, from the seeds she carried in her pack. There were songs that her husband's people had sung to make the corn grow, and she had memorized them. There were signs of rabbits, the lanky long-ears of the dry country. She saw tracks that might indicate deer or, more likely, antelope. Yes, she could do nicely here. Maybe later, after she had become securely one with her medicine-gifts of the spirit, she would move on. Maybe even go home.

But she had continued to postpone that. Travelers passing by stopped to camp, and she found she was able to help and advise, with her herbs and chants and visions. Sometimes, even, with her dream-prophecies, though she avoided foretelling bad events, except in vague terms.

Her fame had spread, and though she knew that people considered her strange, they sought her skills. The years passed, and she became ever more comfortable with her gifts of the spirit, and with this phase of her remarkable life.

So now she watched the distant riders, gauging expertly their rate of travel. Yes, she thought, they should reach her lodge by evening. They would camp nearby. She wondered if they were seeking her skills or if they were merely passing through.

Ah, well, what would be would be. She turned to begin preparing her evening meal.

11

>> >> >>

As the two riders came closer, the medicine woman began to be aware of the nature of their spirits. Sometimes she could tell nothing at all about the travelers who crossed her plain. They were merely people. Sometimes she felt a little. In this case, she was almost overwhelmed by the strength of spirit that emanated from the approaching men. It was a strange spirit, almost frightening. She had not encountered such medicine before.

She could not tell which of the riders might be the one whose spirit reached out. With eyes closed, she tried to identify, to contact this spirit of great power. It was no longer frightening now. That had been only the surprise as she first perceived it. But this was not a spirit that sought to harm, only . . . it was a quest, a seeking thing! Yes, the strength of spirit was driven by a need for something, a search.

She was still having trouble, however. It was such a

mixture. A part of the search seemed to be at odds with another part, or at least distrustful. How could that be, two spirits in one? Suddenly it came to her. She had been trying to relate to one or the other of the riders, to determine which one possessed the powerful spirit that had so startled her. *Aiee*, she thought to herself, it is not one or the other, but both!

Having identified that fact, she was more comfortable. Yes, of course! She could see it now. Two holy men, whose medicines were quite different, had taken the same trail. That in itself was unusual, except that . . . ah, yes . . . their *quests* were similar, and their trails had joined. She wasted no time in trying to determine which medicine was the more powerful. It did not really matter. She was convinced, however, that these two holy men were among the most gifted she had ever met. The spiritual gifts of either man would rival those of the most skilled elders in the kivas of her husband's people. Of course, she had never seen the elders work. Women had been banned from the ceremonies. She still resented that. As one with the gift herself, she could *feel* the events, the powerful forces at work, hidden away in the underground lodges. She could have learned much. . . . Ah, well, that part of her life was behind her.

She turned her attention to the approaching riders again. Yes, they would arrive a little before dark. Shadows were beginning to lengthen, and the two men were near enough now for her to tell more about them.

One rode an exceptionally fine horse. She could tell that before she could determine its color. Strange, how distance made all colors the same. She had noticed that many times. The other animal was unremarkable. It was still some time before they were close enough for her to see that their hairstyles, their garments, and the packs they carried were of different nations. Yes, it was as she had suspected: two entirely different medicines.

Now they were close enough to see the patterns of quill- and beadwork on their shirts and their moccasins. Yes, different. One, the one with the good roan horse, was of the distant plains, the other of the southern mountains. They should know hand signs, then, especially the one from the plains. That would help. Many of the nations of the southwest had not used hand signs, but she had managed to retain the skill, which had been important to her own people.

The tall man on the roan reined in before the spot where she sat and lifted his right hand, palm forward, the sign of peaceable intent. Yes, I was right, she thought with satisfaction. He does use hand signs.

"Greetings, Mother," the man signed. "We saw the smoke of your lodge and would ask to camp here."

It was a logical request. Where there is a dwelling, those who live there must have a source of water, needed for both people and animals.

"How are you called?" she asked.

She could tell by the tall man's smile that he was pleased to find that she could use the hand signs.

"I am Red Horse," he signed. "The other is Digging Owl. We have come far."

She nodded.

"We have a little meat," he offered.

She nodded again. "It is good. There is water in the creek bed. You dig, maybe."

She knew that they would not have to dig. She had cleaned out the sand spring in preparation for their coming, but she wanted to make them appreciate that fact.

"It is good," the traveler signed in return.

He turned his horse in the direction that she had indicated, and the other man followed. She watched, though she tried not to appear that she did so, as they watered the horses, drank, and unsaddled the animals. The horses shook themselves, rolled luxuriously in the sand, shook again, and wandered off to browse along the creek. The two men returned to where she sat, carrying their packs.

"Where?" was the one-sign question from the man who called himself Red Horse. She motioned offhandedly to a level area nearby.

"You may use my fire," she offered.

This was not a simple act of generosity. Fuel was scarce, and if they used her fire, they would gather some sticks, which would in turn reduce *her* chores. She sat and watched while the two foraged for fuel along the stream bed. This took some time, because she had scavenged thoroughly already. By the time they returned, the purple-hued robe of evening was being drawn over the plain. She was cooking some dried corn with some of the meat strips they had offered.

"Owl made a kill a few sleeps ago," Red Horse had explained.

It was good, to have travelers here who had supplies to share.

"How are you called, Mother?" Digging Owl asked as they settled down to eat.

"Ah, I have been called many things," she signed. "New Grass . . . my husband called me Corn Flower . . . sometimes I am called crazy, maybe."

The two men smiled, and this pleased her. They would understand, without the need to explain, her dwelling here on this desolate expanse of plain. But then, these were holy men and should understand.

"What is your nation?" Red Horse asked.

"I have no nation now."

She quickly gave the signs for her own people and that of her husband's.

"I am my own nation," she finished.

The two men nodded without further comment. It was good, she reflected, to have visitors who were men of the spirit themselves. They required no further explanation and asked none. Her location and life-style, which was considered strange by many, was perfectly understandable to these holy men. It was not unlike their quest, she knew, the urge to do or go or stay, without actually knowing why or being able to explain.

They finished eating and settled down to smoke and talk. They gave her a pipeful of tobacco with a pleasant, pungent taste, and she offered in return a mixture of her own, sweetened with strands of fiber from the corn blossom.

They began to exchange stories as the night deepened and the stars multiplied. Creation stories, stories of their own and neighboring nations. There were new stories, ones she had never heard before, and she shared tales that were obviously new to her visitors. It was a pleasant evening, one of more pleasure than she had shared for many seasons.

When the three finally decided to retire, the stars had circled nearly halfway through their nightly arc. The subject of the purpose of the visitors' quest had not arisen. Still, she could not help but wonder.

The men went out into the night a little way to relieve the pressure in their bladders, and she did the same on the opposite side. Then she came back and spread her blanket. She slept outside, as she always did in good weather.

She lay a long time, watching the sky and occasionally glancing at the still forms beyond the fire. She heard the chuckle of the coyotes in the distant darkness, and softer sounds of the night creatures closer at hand. Finally she fell asleep and dreamed.

It was a more vivid and all-encompassing dream than she had experienced for a long time. There were great expanses of the earth involved, and she moved with great rapidity from one place to another. She saw changing weather, drought where there should be rain, and people suffering from hunger.

She awoke once, shaken by the dream, and lay awake in wonder. She renewed the fire and returned to the blanket. The dream was incomplete, and she was not even sure if it was dream or vision. Then it came to her. She must be picking up fragments of the visions of her visitors.

Yes, of course, their quest. It must be because of the hunger and the changing weather patterns. The buffalo . . . she wondered how much *they* knew of this.

She fell asleep quickly this time, hoping to complete the dream. She might even be able to give the two seekers some help on their way. And she dreamed again, strange foreboding dreams this time. There was a great hole in the level plain, and when one looked over the edge there were myriads of buffalo below. The creatures milled about uncertainly. Then there came a terrible darkness. It seemed that a great storm cloud had begun to . . . to *cover the sun!* The day became dark, and the buffalo rushed in terror, crushing each other against the sides of the hole. There were men there, too, and fire thrown from heaven. She did not understand. Buffalo were running frantically past on both sides, and she feared for the safety of the men in front of her. She did not fear for her own safety; she felt above the danger, somehow.

Then she awoke, to wish once more that she had not been cursed with her gifts. At least, some of them. She had, in the short time since she met the two men beyond the fire there, come to like and respect them. They were here, far from home, carrying out their responsibilities as holy men for the good of their people. They knew there was danger, and they were willing to take the risk to bring back the buffalo.

For that must be the quest, the goal they sought together. It was too bad that one of them must die. And she had not even been able to determine which one.

Aiee, this gift was indeed a curse!

12

>> >> >>

She wished she could be more specific with her warning, but it had not been shown to her, which one it would be. Maybe she could make it vague, yet still warn them.

She had wakened with the dread she always felt when her foresight showed her an impending tragedy. This time, somehow, it was worse: the intensity of the spirits of these two holy men, perhaps. Yet with that intensity, it puzzled her a little that she could not tell which of the two must die. Maybe because of their closeness of purpose? Ah, it was no use. Never before had she felt more helpless or more cursed by the possession of her gift. This quest, by two holy men to whom she felt such an affinity, was extremely important. She was certain of that.

The two men rose at dawn, chewed a little of their dried meat, and left some for her as a token of thanks for her hospitality. They saddled their horses and prepared to leave.

"Thank you, Mother," the taller one, Red Horse, said to her. "May your lodge be blessed by good times."

"And yours," she answered. "Both your lodges."

They swung up and turned away.

"Wait!" she called urgently.

The two turned back, questioning. Now that she had begun, she did not know how to proceed.

"May your quest go well—both of you," she said, embarrassed.

They nodded thanks, and she plunged ahead.

"I am made to think," she said carefully, "that you will have success. But the danger . . . that is very great."

The two men looked puzzled.

"You have had a vision? A sign?" Digging Owl asked.

"No. Well, yes . . . but not a clear one."

She hated to withhold information that might be critical.

"Then what—?" Owl demanded.

"There is grave danger . . . more to one than to the other. But I could not see which one. So you must both take care."

They nodded, but she was afraid they were missing the message. After her careful attempt to warn that one would die, without actually saying so, her warning had been reduced to general advice, "You must be careful." It was frustrating, but she did not want to say more. Maybe they understood more than she realized. Ah, well, it was likely that they could not have avoided the danger anyway.

Her vision had been so confusing. Buffalo, a hole in

the ground, brightly colored earth. And the darkness, as clouds seemed to devour the sun. This was a matter of extreme importance, she was sure. But what did it mean?

The two travelers turned away again, and she watched them go, the rising sun painting the left sides of men and horses with a brilliant yellow splash of light. She shook her head in frustration and turned back toward her lodge. Maybe the two, or the one who survived, would come back to tell her of the outcome of the quest.

"That is a strange one," Digging Owl observed as they rode.

The rocky knoll and the lodge of the medicine woman were growing small in the distance behind them. It was the first that either man had spoken.

"Yes," agreed Red Horse. "She sees many things."

"I am made to think so too," Owl said. "She knows much of our quest."

Red Horse nodded and rode silently for a little while. Finally he spoke. "She sees things not given to us," he said flatly.

"I am made to think so. Her warning . . . was that not more than just 'Be careful'?"

"That was my thought too. Maybe she has seen more of our quest than *we* have."

Digging Owl reined his horse to a stop. "Should we go back and ask her?" he asked.

Red Horse stopped also, lost for a moment. "I am made to think not. The woman would have told us, if she could."

He was thinking of the white bull, and how it seemed improper for him to share that part of his vision with Digging Owl. Owl, in turn, had implied that there were parts of *his* vision known only to himself.

"Maybe," Red Horse said thoughtfully, "maybe we have all been given parts of the same vision, but no one has all. The medicine woman sees another part."

"Maybe," Owl agreed. "Maybe she should go with us."

"No. She follows her vision, as we do ours. We have been told to go. If she was told the same, she would be with us. So her vision did not send her with us."

"That is true. It only let her warn us. But we should listen to her warning and be very careful."

"Yes." Red Horse touched the roan with his heel and they moved forward. "I wonder," he said. "Are there others who have parts of the same vision?"

"Maybe so," Digging Owl observed. "We have the same goal, you and I—maybe the medicine woman, too—to bring back the buffalo. That would benefit *every* nation."

Red Horse thought of the owl prophet and his chant, and of the medicine man he had seen when he stopped with a Head Splitter band for a night as he traveled. They had talked little, but the holy man had been performing a ceremony with the burning of pungent herbs as an incense. The clouds of bluish smoke had been most impressive, and the fragrance unique. Had *that* holy man also had a part of the vision that would help them all?

Well, no matter, he decided. A person could be responsible only for his own vision. His was the search for the white bull, and he would carry it out.

During the next few days of travel, the country flattened even more. There was one entire day when they saw not a single landmark to guide by: no distant rocks or hills, no watercourses, only flat, interminable distance. The position of the sun, and of the stars at night, was their only reassurance that they were still on earth and not lost in some otherworld, doomed to wander forever without direction. It was reassuring, when darkness fell, to identify the Seven Hunters and follow their course to the Real-star.

Water was becoming an urgent problem. They were accustomed to the necessity of digging in a dry stream bed to obtain water, but here there were no stream beds, even dry ones, only flat, monotonous plain. It did not look like anything that Red Horse had ever seen, even in his vision. He began to doubt the accuracy of their direction. The horses looked gaunt and listless, sniffing continually, trying to catch the scent of water.

One thing was fortunate. The short curly grass of the western prairie was abundant here. In most places it covered the plain like a spread robe, woolly in appearance. It grew thickly, though no more than a hand's span in height. The horses grazed it eagerly at every opportunity, chewing at the gray-green curls in obvious enjoyment. It was because of this moisture, perhaps, that they seemed not to suffer from thirst as much as their riders. The men tried chewing the grass and found the taste not unpleasant. But the moisture was scant, and it was necessary to spit out the dry residue. No, this was not the answer. Likewise, licking the dew from the grasses in the early morning was pleasant, but hardly worth the effort.

They decided to travel at night, when the air was cooler, to conserve the water they were losing in sweat. During the day, they sat huddled in the shade of their robes or slept in short spells. Both realized that the situation was becoming desperate. Still, they agreed that the signs were right: the direction of the slight breeze, the cry of the coyotes at night, the scream of a hawk as it circled and then sped southward. They must continue, despite any doubts, because they had no alternative. Besides, they already knew what lay behind them: nothing that would be of help, for several days' travel. Discouraged, they plodded on, thirsty and weak.

Finally, the day came when Red Horse was ready to concede that his quest was mistaken. Somehow, he had misunderstood his vision and had gone wrong. The fitful sleep of the day gave little rest, and the two men hardly spoke as they saddled and mounted for the night's ride. There was, in the dim recesses of their minds, the unpleasant suspicion that they would be unable to make another night's journey.

Red Horse dozed fitfully in the saddle, half awake and sometimes dreaming. He thought he was a child again, tied on the back of a dependable old mare, to be lulled to restful sleep by the animal's rocking motion as she grazed. This had long been the custom of his people. It was one of the reasons they had come to be called Elk-dog People. It was also the means of producing the finest riders, hunters, and fighting men on the plains. A child of the People could ride a horse like a warrior almost before he could walk.

Red Horse was not thinking of these things as he slumped and dozed, comforted in a childlike way by the gentle sway of the stallion's gait. He had become in spirit like a child again, had given up the worry and concern. In his despair, he stopped the fight he had been waging against heat, thirst, and hunger, and his mind became receptive again, like . . . like that of a child.

He must have been sound asleep, though not dreaming, when an abrupt change in the rhythm of the horse's motion jerked him back to reality. He woke, glanced at the stars, and realized that they were no longer traveling due south. It was more a southeasterly direction. Impatiently, he pulled the horse's head around. The animal tossed his head, pulling impatiently back toward the southeast. Red Horse jerked on the rein, irritated at the misbehavior. Such a well-trained horse should not be expected to behave in this way, and the roan had never done so before . . . well, just once at the dry stream bed, when he had scented water.

Water! Could it be? Were the horse's fine-tuned senses telling him something not recognized by mere humans? Red Horse let the rein go slack, and the roan headed eagerly to the southeast, quickening his walking step. The rider glanced over his shoulder, to see the other horse following. Digging Owl was still slumped over, apparently asleep.

It was only a little distance, no more than a few hundred paces. The horse pricked up his ears and nickered softly. There in the dim starlight ahead was the most beautiful sight in the world: the reflection of stars on a smooth, glassy stretch of water. Three antelope, disturbed at the water's edge, floated away and disappeared like gray ghosts in the mists of darkness.

"Owl! Wake up!" Red Horse tried to shout, but his cry emerged more like a husky whisper.

The rider tumbled from the saddle as the roan stopped and stretched his neck to drink. He landed in shallow water, with mud underneath. It was soft and warm and life-giving. On hands and knees, he took a sip, then another, sloshing the fluid around in his mouth. He raised his head to look for Digging Owl. The other man was on his knees in the water too, splashing his face as he dipped to drink double hand-fuls from his cupped palms.

Owl looked up and laughed. "I do not know how you did this, my brother, but it is good! Your medicine is powerful."

Red Horse laughed too. He could take credit for this miracle, and under some circumstances he might have. But this was too important an event.

"*Aiee!*" he cried. "It is not my medicine, friend, but that of my borrowed horse!"

"It is still good," Owl retorted. "Your horse has more powerful medicine than either of us!"

Both laughed again, like little children. Then Owl became serious.

"This sign is good . . . very good," he said. "We *are* on the right trail, after all."

So Digging Owl had had his doubts, too. It was com-forting to Red Horse that he was not alone. But he was embarrassed to think he had doubted his spirit-guide.

"What is this water?" Owl asked. "Not a stream?"

"I think not," Horse answered. "A buffalo wallow, maybe. We will see in the morning."

They crawled from the water, stripped the saddles and packs from the horses, and lay down to sleep, only a few steps from the water's edge. It was their best sleep in many days.

13
>> >> >>

The buffalo wallow was less than a stone's throw across. The depth of the water would hardly reach a man's knees at any point, but at the time and place, it had been lifesaving. They camped there for a day, resting and recovering.

In the relief at finding water, it was sometime later before they really began to consider how it had happened. A mudhole in the midst of a high, dry prairie as flat as a sheet of ice? It seemed unlikely, when Red Horse thought of it, but there it was. Owl was even more puzzled. The two sprawled near the water shortly after daylight, still resting, feeling the rejuvenation of the water to their thirsty bodies. The horses grazed hungrily a short distance away. Already, the condition of the animals was visibly improved.

"Tell me," Digging Owl asked. "Are these water holes found in your country?"

"Yes, sometimes. My country is more rolling hills."

"You called this . . . last night . . . a buffalo place?"

"Yes. Our people say the buffalo make this hole to catch rainwater where there are no streams."

Owl seemed astonished. "They paw out the dirt?"

His was a country of sand, which would not hold water in such a basin, and of scattered bunchgrass rather than this curly layer of shortgrass that robed the plain.

"Yes," Red Horse related. "Some of the wallows have been there for many lifetimes. Who knows when or how they started? A little rain falls, and there is mud; the buffalo drinks, then rolls in the mud to keep the flies from biting him."

"Yes, that would help," Digging Owl agreed.

"But that is not all," Horse continued. He reached out and plucked a tiny seed stalk from the grass near him. "See, the seeds are very small. When the animal rolls around and is covered with mud, there will be some seeds in his mud coat. Then he runs—a day, maybe more, a long way. . . . The mud dries and falls off, and new seed is planted."

"Ah!" exclaimed Owl excitedly. "He plants his own grass!"

"Yes. We call it the buffalo grass. This is part of the medicine of the buffalo . . . *my* medicine. These are the things I learned from my father, the holy man."

Owl was deep in thought. "Horse," he said, "we have talked of the story in both our nations, that of the hole where the buffalo entered the world."

"Yes?"

"And I have seen this in my vision, though not clearly."

"Yes, so you have said."

"I wonder . . . could these—the buffalo wallows,

you call them—are *these* the holes, now plugged with mud?"

It was a sobering thought. Was this the origin, not only of the buffalo but of the shortgrass that nourished him over much of his range? Red Horse stared at the wallow in wonderment. He had never heard such a theory. Surely, there would have been something in the legends of the People.

"I do not think so," he said slowly, "but let us stay here a day. We can both pray and seek advice, while we try to feel the spirit of this place."

Owl readily agreed. It would be good for the horses, too, to have a day to graze and renew their strength. The men continued to discuss the possibilities from time to time.

"Where did this water come from, in the buffalo hole?" Digging Owl wondered. "From below?"

"In my country, it would be rain," Horse observed.

"But would rain not leak out?" Owl persisted.

"It would go away, in a few days, but not leak out. See this mud? It is much better than sand for holding water."

Owl nodded. "But, even so, there must have been a rain to fill it."

"Yes, I suppose so. Maybe in the last four or five sleeps," Horse agreed.

"And there must be rain to feed this grass."

"Of course. What—?"

"I do not know," Owl said thoughtfully. "I was only thinking out loud. Maybe we are nearing a good place for buffalo. Here is grass, water—"

"But where are they?"

"I am made to think again of the hole in the ground, where the buffalo came out," Owl said.

"But, in your vision—you said that you saw it. Did it look like *this?*"

Red Horse knew he was coming perilously close to asking of another's medicine, but Owl seemed to realize the urgency of the question.

"No." He considered. "That is what troubles me, Horse. In my vision, the hole looked nothing like this, nothing at all."

"Then you—"

"I am made to think," Owl interrupted, "that this, a good *place* for buffalo, is only a sign. We are on the right trail."

Red Horse thought for a little while. "It may be. We have had few signs for a while, unless this is one."

"Yes. You noticed there is some buffalo sign here?" Owl pointed to a dry and crumbling buffalo chip.

"Yes, but it is old. Let us wait a little."

Just at dusk the three antelope returned to drink. Red Horse, watching the stallion, saw the little ears prick forward as the animal raised his head, curious. There, only a few steps away, stood the graceful ghosts of the dry plains, where there had been nothing a moment ago. He held his breath, frozen motionless, lest he frighten them away. Digging Owl was reaching for his bow. . . .

The antelope suddenly sprang away for no apparent reason: a stray scent on a puff of breeze, maybe, or a chance motion that gave warning. In a few graceful leaps they had vanished. Red Horse turned to look at his companion. Far from disappointment, Digging Owl was smiling broadly.

"Did you see?" he cried eagerly. "They ran south, straight south! There is our sign!"

Red Horse had not realized that fact, but it was true.

And they were not in desperate need of meat. As Owl had realized, the importance of the antelope was not as the replenishment of supplies, but as the sign they sought. Red Horse was slightly embarrassed at having missed the significance, but Owl seemed not to notice. Anyway, Horse told himself, his was the medicine of the buffalo, not antelope. Even so, he thought, he should have realized—

"It is good." Owl interrupted his thoughts. "Our quest goes well."

Three days later, they had cause to wonder again. Their waterskins were empty, and they had found no more. They camped at a buffalo wallow similar to the last, except that it was dry. Only sun-baked mud appeared in the bottom of the depression, fissured and split into hundreds of geometric designs as it had dried. Digging Owl persisted in prying around in the caked chunks of dry mud. He wished to test his theory of the plugged buffalo hole.

"No," he finally decided, "it is as you say. The bottom is solid."

He seemed disappointed. But the real disappointment was for lack of needed water. The horses stood sniffing and pawing in vain at the dry depression.

"I will perform a ceremony," said Digging Owl.

"Ceremony?"

"A dance . . . to bring rain."

He said no more, but spread his robe and fell asleep quickly. Red Horse lay awake, wondering about the rain ceremony of his companion. He knew that nations in the drier regions had medicine that allowed them to ask for rain. His own medicine was more for the foretelling. Well, he would see. It was strange country to both men.

Red Horse woke at dawn, aroused by the rhythmic chant of Owl's rain ceremony. He watched, fascinated, while the gyrating dance and the rising and falling of the chanted song stirred a primitive mood within him. Owl had stripped to the waist and painted himself with geometric designs unfamiliar to Horse. There were arrows, jagged stripes suggestive of Rain Maker's spears of real-fire, and slanting lines that without much imagination could represent rain. There were rattles at his knees, made of antelope hoofs or some similar material, and he carried a larger gourd rattle in his hand. From time to time, he would stoop and pick up a handful of dirt from the dry wallow, never missing the rhythmic beat of his chant. He would hold the dust skyward and then fling it with a sweeping gesture, to drift back to earth through the still air.

Red Horse was fascinated. His own rain dance depended on timing. As an apprentice, he had been firmly taught that one does not attempt the rain dance when the signs are completely negative. The holy man must have something to work with. He was certain that Digging Owl must take much the same approach, but what signs of rain had there been? It was easy to think that the medicine of Owl was stronger than his own. But was it true? The gifts of each were attuned to the spirits of their own countries. This area was known to neither but was more nearly like that of Digging Owl, at least as far as the coming of rain.

Horse assumed that rain in this place would come from the southwest, as it did in the Sacred Hills. That was a well-known summer pattern. Consequently, he was watching in that direction. He saw nothing, beyond the flat expanse of the plain, illuminated strangely by the rising sun behind him. Maybe . . .

maybe a hint of distant clouds along earth's rim? No, that might be hills or mountains, many days away, a thin gray-blue line against the brighter blue of sky. He turned his attention back to the dancer.

Digging Owl continued his ceremony, seemingly oblivious to all else. He did not even look around the horizon. To the earth, to the sky, but not to the far distance. Red Horse glanced there again. Was it—could it be that in the center of the blue line there was a heavier bulge? He tried to remember how it had looked the last time he glanced that way.

In a short while, there was no doubt. The cloud bank was thickening, rising, moving toward them. Digging Owl continued his chant a little longer and then paused, exhausted. He stood with Red Horse, watching the storm grow. It was not a large rain cloud, but fast-moving. There was the flicker of orange fire within the gray of the cloud. It seemed a long time before he could hear the distant mutter of Rain Maker's drum rolling across the prairie.

The cloud swept forward, expanding, dividing, breaking in pieces that seemed to drop their load of moisture and vanish. From time to time he saw patterns in the storm, lines slanting diagonally from a low-hanging cloud to the plain below. Sometimes Rain Maker hurled his spears of real-fire through the falling rain, to crash against the earth, followed by the drum rumble. There was a remarkable similarity between the gray-blue and yellow designs of the distant storm and the gray-blue and yellow designs on the chest, arms, and back of Digging Owl.

There was a shorter time, now, between the flash of real-fire and the crash of the rain drum. Red Horse was becoming anxious. It was known that one should not stand in the open, attracting the attention of Rain

Maker as he selected targets for his spears. At least there were no cottonwood trees, noted for attracting Rain Maker's unwanted attention.

Now Digging Owl stood to his full height and raised his arms skyward in a challenge to the storm. It seemed a foolish thing, but if one is to bring a rain, he must do something to attract it. It was merely one of the dangers of Owl's duties as a holy man.

Nevertheless, Horse shrank from this exposure. His medicine did not include taking such risks. He edged away from Owl. He was unwilling to accept the danger of an accidental injury to himself in case of a near miss by a thrown spear of real-fire. He was concerned about the horses but could do nothing, as the storm raced toward them. The front edge of the falling rain could be plainly seen in its advance, approaching faster than a horse could run. He could see the fat drops striking dusty ground, stirring the grasses for a moment before that line was obliterated by the downpour.

Then the rain swept over them, and he could see nothing beyond an arm's length. How different, he thought, to observe the patterns and designs from a distance and then to be *inside* the storm, wet and cold and unable to see. Dimly, he watched the splatter of the downpour splashing into the dry mud of the wallow. But it was not dry mud now. It was wet, soggy, being quickly inundated as the depression filled.

Then, as suddenly as it had swept in, the storm was gone and the sky was clearing to the west. It was not yet midmorning. The horses wandered up to drink from the water-filled depression. Digging Owl stood, exhausted, the last remains of his body paint still trickling down his back and legs.

"*Aiee,* my friend," said Red Horse, "yours is a powerful medicine!"

14
>> >> >>

The storm had washed the prairie, and the rain made all the difference the travelers could imagine. It was refreshing merely to fill the lungs with clean, moisture-laden air. After Digging Owl had rested from the physical and spiritual exertion of the rain ceremony, they filled their waterskins. Men and horses drank deeply, all they could hold, and then moved on.

Sun Boy's torch sparkled from droplets on every blade of grass, the sky was a clear washed blue, and the world was good. It was distracting from their quest, almost, so tempting to stop, relax, and enjoy. Surely, it seemed, such beauty, such lush grazing, should tempt the buffalo back to the plains. But they saw none. It was possible, of course, that Owl's rainstorm was very limited in size. It had been a small cloud. Red Horse would have asked about it, but somehow it seemed inappropriate, an intrusion on the privacy of the other's spirit-world. They rode on, saying little.

Another concern began to nag quietly at Red Horse. The more he considered it, the more he worried. He had not thought of it at first, when his quest began. In essence, the problem dealt with the passing of the seasons. In usual times, the great herds had grazed through the country of the People twice each season. The coming of autumn found the herds migrating south to warmer areas to winter. They would return in the spring with the Moon of Greening, to follow the advance of that season on to the north for the summer. Some animals usually remained in the Sacred Hills for the summer, fattening on the lush tallgrass growth.

He tried to apply these well-known facts to the present situation. The widespread drought had distorted the seasons, possibly confusing the buffalo in their herd-spirit travels. The herds would have followed the route that offered the best grazing. When they found it, they would continue with whatever and wherever seemed good.

Now, in the quest of the two holy men, suppose they did find the herds. Would not the time be wrong? Their goal was to bring the herds back northward to the plains, but . . . *aiee*, it would soon be time for migration *south!*

He thought about this at some length. The Sun Dance had been in the Moon of Roses. That Moon had passed during his travels, and most of the Moon of Thunder. It was confusing, because the seasons had been upside down for a year or more. It was almost the Red Moon, as nearly as he could tell. If they found the herds, and by the combined efforts of their two medicines managed to start the animals northward, it must be soon. Surely the seasons would revert to normal soon. If they did, the coming of autumn in the Moon of Ripening would start the herds turning back southward.

There was very little time. They must locate the buffalo quickly and do whatever they must, for there was no possibility of moving the herds *against* the progress of the seasons.

Day by day, this concern weighed more heavily on Red Horse. He wondered if Digging Owl felt it too. Probably. Owl's medicine was strong; the rain ceremony had convinced Horse of that. He longed to discuss the question of passing moons with Owl, but hesitated. It might be important not to express doubt in their mission. So they rode on, avoiding that subject which was of greatest importance.

The country had not changed much since the rain a few days ago. It was still flat, covered with shortgrass, but becoming progressively more dry, the growth more scant. They were beginning to think again of the need for water.

Then came a day when a change caught the undivided attention of both men. Digging Owl saw it first. The afternoon was hot, the horses tired, the men even more so. Red Horse was half dozing to the gentle sway of the roan stallion's gait, when Owl pulled his horse to a stop with a surprised grunt. Instantly, Red Horse was awake.

"What is it?"

"Look!" Owl pointed to the ground.

There, in the direction they were traveling, was the faint suggestion of a worn path. It was hard to trace, and could have been merely a trick of the imagination, but no; it *was* there. Wandering, whimsically detouring around a patch of shortgrass, wavering in direction but returning to the general course . . .

south! One had to be alert to have even noticed it, and then it was easy to doubt. Was it a chance pattern that merely *resembled* a wandering animal trail?

They moved on, watching closely. Another dim suggestion of a path or trail joined this one, and it became plainer to follow. By the time their shadows began to lengthen with the lowering of Sun's torch, there was no longer any doubt. It was unquestionably a trail, made by the repetitive tramp of hundreds or thousands of feet. But feet of what, or whom? Men on foot, whose moccasins left very little sign but wore away the grass? Buffalo? Antelope? Or horses?

They dismounted and walked for some distance, leading the horses, one on each side of the trail so as not to disturb any tracks. There seemed to be none, anyway, but finally Owl grunted and pointed once more. It was not a track but a dried buffalo chip, a pace away from the path. This would seem to indicate, then, that at least some travelers on this trail had been buffalo. It was hard to determine how long the sign had been there.

"There is grass of this year's growth under it," observed Red Horse.

"Yes, but the grass also curls up *over* it," Owl pointed out. "At one point, through it."

This meant that at least one buffalo had traveled this trail since the Moon of Growing, but at least a moon or two ago. They moved on.

"Look, another!" Digging Owl pointed eagerly.

"And on this side!" Red Horse announced his discovery.

The buffalo chips appeared to be of different ages, some dry and falling to powder, others dropped scarcely a moon ago.

"Which way do they travel?" asked Owl.

"I cannot tell," Horse answered.

There flashed through his mind the vision of Owl and the hole in the ground. Could it be that all the buffalo in the world were gathering and reentering the hole? Were these droppings those of the last few animals on earth? It was a sobering thought.

Red Horse shook his head to clear it of such negative ideas. If that were true, his own vision of the white bull would not be so plain. No, it must be something else, some temporary condition . . . weather, whatever. But he continued to question the direction of travel. Most trails lead in both directions. But this one, with other small branches joining it, like streams flowing together to form a larger river? Well, it could be used in either direction, but the pattern seemed to flow southward. They discussed this at length around a campfire that evening—a campfire of dried buffalo chips, which were becoming quite numerous by the time they stopped for the night.

"I am made to think," said Red Horse, "that the buffalo followed this path toward some purpose, some goal."

"I too," Owl agreed. "The Hole-in-the-Earth, maybe?"

"Maybe . . . but *why?*"

Owl shook his head. "They usually follow grass and water," he noted. "But last season there was little grass, little rain. Maybe the grazing is better back inside the ground."

"But the grass is good, here."

"Maybe not last year, or this spring. This is new growth."

"That is true. Do you think they do not *know* that the grass is good again?" Horse persisted.

Owl's eyes became large and round. "And maybe our mission is to *tell* them?"

"Maybe . . . but would they not discover it for themselves?"

Owl chuckled. "If they had, we would not be here!" he said.

Red Horse smiled, at the same time wondering if the weather had normalized at home and if the Sacred Hills were becoming lush and green again. One thing was certain: they were following the trail of increasingly more animals now than they had been earlier. That could mean only one thing. They were now closer to whatever had brought the buffalo. They were closer to their own goal and to the fulfillment of their mission.

Which was . . . what? Though Red Horse had his duty in mind in a general way, the details were definitely not plain. And even more vague were the responsibilities of Digging Owl. Horse still wondered whether their objectives would be in conflict when the time came.

"I am made to think," he observed cautiously, "that whatever place the buffalo have gone is not far away."

"I too," said Owl, as solemn as his namesake.

Sun Boy had just carried his torch to his lodge on the other side. There was still a blaze of color in the western sky.

"Sun Boy chooses his paints well tonight," observed Red Horse.

"Sun Boy?" asked Owl.

"Yes . . . our Sun Boy carries a torch across the sky. Is it not the same with you?"

"Something like that," Owl agreed. "Our deity throws a ball of fire."

"It is good," agreed Horse. "Our Sun Boy's torch

almost goes out each winter. He battles with Cold
Maker, is pushed far south, but gets a new torch and
comes back strong again."

Owl nodded, with a smile. It was a good story. Red
Horse felt a little more comfortable. Surely, a holy
man so companionable, so understanding, would be
nothing to fear when the coming crisis reached its
completion. He glanced to the west again, appreciat-
ing the vivid colors as they faded to a sameness of blue-
gray clouds, each gilded at the edges with a brilliant
light. Then he saw what he had overlooked until now.
More properly, the object had been invisible in the
brighter glare of Sun's torch. It was the new moon, low
in the west, the tiniest sliver of light against the darkening gray of the heavens. The outline of the rest of
the moon's circle could be seen, even darker than the
sky behind.

He spoke softly to his companion. "Look!"

"Yes," said Digging Owl, equally moved. "Is this a
sign for us?"

"Maybe . . . but a sign of what?"

"I do not know," Owl said, almost in a whisper.
"But, my friend, this is powerful medicine. Maybe our
quest is almost over."

"I am made to think so too," Red Horse agreed.

They sat awake, a long time. Both seemed to feel
that sleeping was out of the question. The spirit of the
night was so powerful that if one slept, he might miss
something of great importance. Together, they sat and
watched the thin splinter of the moon slide silently
behind earth's rim. Even deeper darkness overspread
the plain, broken only by the innumerable points of
light scattered across heaven's dome like distant
campfires.

In the distance, a coyote called to his mate.

15
>> >> >>

Next morning, some of the magic and mystery was gone. But then, things of the spirit usually seem closer with the coming of darkness under the open skies. The two men rose and prepared to go on. Little was said, but there was still an excitement in the air, a promise of impending events.

The signs of buffalo were more frequent. Now and then they noticed the unmistakable track of a cloven hoof in the dried mud of the trail. There were droppings, too, that appeared quite fresh. Some grasses seemed recently grazed.

But beyond that, nothing. Toward noon, they stopped for a brief rest, puzzled that there was nothing ahead but flat, uninhabited plain as far as eye could see. Surely, they should see *something*.

"We can see for three sleeps ahead," Red Horse pointed out, "yet there is only more of this!"

Owl nodded, equally puzzled. "But we have this

trail," he said. "It grows broader and seems closer to
. . . whatever lies ahead."

It was obvious that he, too, was searching for answers. Red Horse noted that, as fast as the buffalo
could move, it would take three days for them to be
out of sight on this plain. Most puzzling was that there
were now droppings that seemed fresher than three
days. *Aiee*, what a mystery!

"The direction still seems right," Digging Owl observed, "and the trail plain."

"That is true," Horse agreed, "but where can it go?
We should see this broad a trail plainly, far ahead!
Unless . . ."

The two looked at each other in open-mouthed disbelief.

"Unless it goes into the ground." Owl finished the
unspoken thought. "The Hole-in-the-Earth . . . it is
as my vision said!"

Red Horse felt the hair on the back of his neck begin
to prickle. His skin felt cold, even in the heat of the
day.

This was a thing of powerful medicines, of the very
forces of Creation, maybe. It could be dangerous, yet
they could not turn back. The future of both their
nations depended on the ability of the two holy men to
deal with this crisis.

Red Horse was still quite confused over this new
development. Why had his own vision had nothing to
do with a hole in the ground, into which buffalo had
disappeared? Why was that given only to Digging
Owl? He had to confess that he was still having a great
deal of trouble with the entire idea of this hole. And
yet it seemed the only explanation for what they saw
before them.

Then a miracle seemed to happen before their very

eyes. His glance caught the suggestion of motion in front of them, and he turned his head to look. There, maybe two or three bow shots away, a dark form rose, directly out of the surface of the earth. Through the consternation of being witness to such a thing, Red Horse tried to observe all that he could about the phenomenon. The first visible object was the head of a large buffalo cow—an old cow, it seemed, from the appearance of her horns and her attitude. She seemed wary yet aggressive, a cow typical of the leaders of any herd. Her hump rose, too, and she lurched forward, pulling herself upward with her front feet, up out of . . . out of the Hole-in-the-Earth.

The cow stood entirely on the plain now. She looked around and seemed not to notice the two riders, probably because they were not moving, and the buffalo's distant vision is notoriously poor. It was helpful, too, that the breeze put the riders downwind. Red Horse noted with satisfaction that some things held true, even in such a supernatural situation.

The roan stallion had scented buffalo now and pricked his ears forward, ready for the chase. With some difficulty, Red Horse restrained him. They must observe this thing which was being shown to them.

"Look! Her calf!" Owl pointed.

The yellowish calf, of this year's generation, came bobbing up, dancing around its mother, leaping and bucking with the joy of young things in the sunshine of a pleasant day.

Next there appeared a young cow, perhaps the old leader's calf of the previous season. Then another cow, sniffing the air, and a young bull.

The riders could smell the animals now, the breeze being from the south, blowing from the buffalo toward them. The scent was stronger, though, than one would expect from these few individuals at this distance. It was more like the scent one experiences at the beginning of a hunt. It was not the scent of individual animals, which may be too slight to notice. This was the smell of a great herd, the combined smell of hundreds or thousands. There were mixed scents of sweat, dust, manure, and the distinctive smell of the animals themselves. It was the herd smell, the exciting yet indescribable odor that causes the hunter's palms to sweat as he holds the bow and drives the buffalo horse into an impatient frenzy.

"The buffalo—the great herd!" said Owl softly. "The hole. . . ."

Red Horse nodded numbly. He realized now that he had never really believed the theory of the Hole-in-the-Earth. The original story, maybe, the Creation story, but not that the herds had gone *back* down the hole. He had seen and experienced many things beyond the understanding of mere humans, but this . . . *aiee!* He could even hear the bellowing challenge of a distant bull, still unseen below the surface.

He was confused; his senses not ready for this. He was still reluctant to believe what he was seeing, hearing, even smelling. Yet there it was, plainly before him. He could no longer deny it. Even as he hesitated, another animal came thrusting head and shoulders upward into the sunlight of the plain.

"Owl, I must see the hole," he mumbled, kneeing his horse forward.

The stallion tried to run and was confused and frustrated when Red Horse circled and pulled him in. Finally he quieted, and they moved forward nervously. They were within a bow shot when the wary old cow gave a snort of alarm and turned back. One of the younger animals trotted to the spot where they had first appeared and simply slipped back over the rim and out of sight. Both men gasped.

"They must not go back!" Digging Owl whispered with alarm.

"They came out," Red Horse said. "They will come out again."

Very slowly, they rode nearer and then reined in, amazed at what lay before them. They stood almost on the rim of a great canyon, which seemed to widen and stretch into the far distance. There, the distant plain had merged in their perception with the plain on which they stood. For several days, as they traveled and looked ahead, they had been looking *across* this great rift in the earth, across to the other side.

And below, far below, were the buffalo. Hundreds, thousands, grazing peacefully.

"This is as I saw it," said Digging Owl simply. "The hole."

Red Horse felt stupid, embarrassed. Somehow, his imagination had envisioned a hole not much larger than to admit one animal. Of course, a great herd would require a great hole, or cleft, like this. He had simply been mistaken, had tried to force his thoughts into a pattern that did not fit. He must be more ready to *accept* and not try to *explain.*

He could see plainly, now, the illusion that had encouraged his mistake. In various places along the rim, a steep trail climbed the canyon wall. Buffalo must wander up these trails to graze on the upper flat and return to the canyon . . . of course! There must be a stream, or springs, below. They would go back down to water. The riders had chanced to see a few animals as they hauled themselves up and over the canyon rim. He smiled to himself at the deception.

He saw the entire problem more clearly now. In a

time of severe drought, this great herd had found a place that had escaped. There was grass here, and water, and they had stayed, rather than venture to migrate across parched grassland. Now the shortgrass had returned, but the buffalo were still reluctant, especially since conditions were good here. There might be other such areas here in the southern plains. Not on so grand a scale as this, perhaps, but enough to account for where the herds had gone. *Aiee!* The Hole-in-the-Earth! It was true! Red Horse had simply been unaware of the nature of the hole. He chuckled to himself again.

"It is as I saw it," Owl said. "Bigger, maybe. Now we must get them out."

Horse would have laughed except that Digging Owl was dead serious. Owl had come all this way with a singleness of purpose, and the ultimate task was plain. Somehow, Owl felt, they must encourage the herd to move up, out of the "hole" and back to their normal migration patterns. Only in this way would the many nations of the plains, with all their scattered bands, have a return to reliable food supplies. Red Horse wondered if Owl's vision had shown him how to accomplish this. The gnawing doubt began to return. Were they to compete? Would it be a contest of medicines, in a race for the white bull of his vision? He must approach this cautiously, for he had seen the power of the other man's medicine in the rain ceremony.

"Does your vision tell you how to do this thing?" Red Horse asked.

Digging Owl looked up sharply, suspiciously. "Does yours?" he demanded.

The question was, in effect, an accusation, a statement that this was too private a question. It was an intrusion on the secrets of another's medicine.

"Forgive me, brother," Horse stammered. "I only meant . . . are we to work together?"

He had not answered the question, and neither had Owl, and it hung there between them, a barrier to progress—to conversation, even. There was distrust, and both felt it. They were farther apart than when their journey began. So Owl, too, wondered whether their medicine would be in conflict.

"I am made to think," Digging Owl said carefully, "that we should each go his own way."

"It is good," said Red Horse.

It was not good. The taste of this was like ashes in his mouth. The two had come far together. Possibly neither could have succeeded alone, without the support of the other. It had appeared that this was meant to be, that the two had a common goal. But now that they had arrived, distrust had surfaced again. It would make it impossible for them to work together, to share their medicines.

"Shall we camp together tonight and part when day comes?" Red Horse suggested.

Owl nodded, pointed to a spot near the rim, and began to unsaddle. Red Horse, doing the same, longed to tell his companion of the white bull and of what he was called to do.

The two men picketed their horses, because of the unpredictable nature of buffalo, and retired by a small fire of chips. They spoke very little. Actually, they slept very little, too. There was excitement in the air. Red Horse tossed and turned, watching the slow arc of the Seven Hunters as they circled the Real-star. From time to time he listened to the lowing murmur of the herd below and the distant call of coyotes. Once there was the deeper cry of one of the big wolves that follow the herds.

There was one other thing, a thing that disturbed him. As he sat up, along toward morning, to rearrange his robe, he saw a point of light on the distant plain beyond the herd. It was like a distant campfire, perhaps a day's journey away. Then it was gone. He looked again, but it did not return.

Were there yet others who camped here, preparing to invoke their own medicine gifts?

16

>> >> >>

When Red Horse awoke, the gray light of dawn was lying over the earth, lending an eerie feeling to the coming day. He turned to find his companion nowhere at hand. Quickly, he rose, mildly alarmed. Where had the man gone?

It took only a moment. Digging Owl's robe, his pack, horse, and saddle—all were nowhere to be seen. Owl had been quite serious in his suggestion that they should part, and he had initiated the move.

Red Horse viewed this with strangely mixed emotions. One does not easily part with a companion who has shared hardships and hopes. He would have liked to say something in parting. On the other hand, there had been that barrier between them last night, the thin layer of distrust that had made them both uncomfortable. Their goals were similar but not quite the same, maybe.

No, it was better to have parted this way. Each

could pursue his own trail and carry out his own medicine, which would be slightly different. The shared part of their quest was over, and it had been good. It had accomplished the shared part of their purpose. Together, they had found the location of the great herd, of Owl's Hole-in-the-Earth. . . . Horse smiled again at how he himself had failed to understand the nature of the hole.

Now each could pursue a different trail. He knew little of the trail Digging Owl would take. Owl had mentioned, and only briefly, the necessity to in some way move the herd out of the canyon and back onto the plains. That was true, of course, but how? Maybe Owl had some idea, some medicine or ceremony that he would carry out.

Ah, well, no matter. The thing that now faced Red Horse was his own trail. He must fulfill his part in this complex situation. And that was as mysterious as ever. He had had no indication at all of what he must do, beyond the one vision of the white bull. His feelings, after searching the Story Skins for their secrets, had been that he must somehow restore to the People the white cape that seemed to have so much significance. But obviously, before he could fashion and use the white buffalo cape, he must find, kill, and skin the white bull. That seemed, at this point, an overwhelming goal. In all his life, he had never even seen a white buffalo—except, of course, in his vision.

He walked over to the canyon's rim and watched the thousands of shaggy creatures below. As the day brightened, he could distinguish individual animals more easily, and he studied them carefully. There was, of course, some variation in color. Most of the animals were dark brown, almost black, with the calves of this season lighter in color, a soft reddish-yellow. Here and there, an individual animal was somewhat lighter brown, and occasionally one that was almost tawny, though that was rare. He remembered having seen a young cow once, years before, that was almost mouse-colored, a bluish-gray. Someone . . . he could not remember . . . someone in the Northern band, maybe, was the proud owner of a robe of similar color.

But white? Had such a thing ever been? Maybe the pigments on the ancient Story Skins were only an approximation, and the sacred cape had been merely light-colored. But no, his vision had been plain enough. His search was for a *white* bull.

The impossibility of this quest nearly overwhelmed him. Below were thousands. Must he sort these creatures, like so many grains of sand, for the lightest to be found?

Why me? he wondered silently, staring glumly at the herd below. Some animals were grazing; others were lying down, calmly chewing grass ingested earlier. It was a peaceful scene, but he knew that if the proper event stimulated excitement, the canyon floor would become a dangerous melee of rushing dark bodies. And it appeared that it would be necessary for him to descend into the canyon—the "hole." He did not relish the thought.

A coyote wandered along the rim, coming toward him at a leisurely pace, seeming to ignore his presence. He paid little attention. The creature was probably looking for a way down the cliff's face, to search for scraps left after the ever-circling buffalo wolves pulled down a weak or injured animal. Horse glanced at the coyote again. It had stopped, a few paces away, and was sitting, watching *him*. The remarkable thing was the expression on the animal's face. It was a quizzical, almost humorous thing, almost as if . . . well, as if the creature were laughing at him. Then it rose, turned, and slipped silently over the rim, onto one of the nebulous paths that snaked along the face of the cliff wall.

Too late, he realized. *Aiee!* How could he have failed to see? He ran to the edge, where the coyote had disappeared, and looked over, but there was no sign. *Aiee!* To be so stupid as not to have recognized his own spirit-guide!

"I am sorry, Grandfather!" he pleaded, but there was no response.

He sat down, dejected. He was unsure of his next step and felt he had missed his chance to be shown the way. Why should his spirit-guide torment him in this manner? Very slowly, he calmed and began again to consider his situation. It would be unlikely that he could receive any help if his mind was occupied with worry and anxiety.

As he calmed, realization dawned upon him. The guidance he sought had already been offered, and he had not recognized it. His guide . . . of course! The coyote had come along the rim of the gorge, much as he had himself. Then, after pausing to attempt to communicate, the guide had slipped over the edge to descend to the floor of the canyon.

It was quite plain. He must, after his observation from the top, descend into the gorge himself, to make personal contact with the herd-spirit of the buffalo. It was, perhaps, the same principle as the apology for a kill, but in reverse. After the kill, the hunter apologizes to the spirits of all buffalo, everywhere, through this one which lies dead at his feet. In this case, Horse was coming to see, he must renew his spiritual contact with the herd. He must return to his days as an apprentice, to his vision-quest, and must try to reenter the thoughts of the buffalo, to get inside their heads.

Only in this way would he be able to locate the white bull—if, indeed, there was such an animal. Maybe the whole thing was a matter of the spirit, and the white bull did not exist on an earthly level. But the Story Skins were quite plain. They depicted a cape made from such an animal.

Well, no matter, he decided, as he rose. He would fast . . . yes, that would be good. Owl had been right to separate. This situation demanded a rebirth, of a sort. It was, in effect, a second vision-quest, for which one would fast. He would postpone his descent into the gorge until his first day of fasting was over and he began to attain the clarity of the senses that he sought.

He rebuilt the small fire, which had died to white dust, and offered a tiny piece of dried meat to the spirits of the place. He sang a song to the morning and then walked on foot along the canyon's rim, to observe the herd below and the possible trails he might use to descend. He found several, but deferred any decision for now. This activity merely helped to pass the time, to get through the temporary period of fasting when the hunger pangs interfere with things of the spirit. He gave the horse a little water from his waterskin, promising more.

"We will go down to water tomorrow, my brother."

Then he picketed the roan in a new, ungrazed spot and returned to observe the herd. The canyon, he saw, was gouged out of the level plain, narrow at the upper end but broadening rapidly as it opened onto the plain below. The floor of the canyon was irregular at this point, a broken series of hillocks and rolling grassy slopes. But very soon, it became a plain of its own, merging with the slightly rolling grassland beyond, the plain they had been observing for several days. He noted that the area was heavily grazed, which ac-

counted for the forays up and onto the plateau, by
small bands such as he and Owl had witnessed. It was
good. If the grass was becoming scarce, it would be
easier to persuade the herds to resume their normal
migration patterns.

Aside from the herd itself, the most striking thing
about the canyon was the great beauty of the place.
There were colors, shifting and changing as the morning sun's rays probed into its depths, beyond anything
he had ever seen before. Bright greens, of unfamiliar
trees and shrubs along the canyon wall, contrasted
with earth colors in stone and shale and soil. Each
hillock that rose above the canyon floor had its own
pattern of horizontal stripes, layers of color that went
entirely around, or maybe through, the formations.
There were narrow bands of red, yellow, gray-blue,
and brown. This would be a marvelous place to dig
pigments for paint, he thought. There were colors
here he had never seen.

Even more remarkable, maybe, was that the same
sequence repeated itself over and over. He could
identify a stripe of yellowish pigment, between two of
red-brown, that appeared in a hillock below him.
Then, in a formation a bow shot away to the southwest, the same combination of stripes appeared, at
apparently the same level. And beyond that, the yellow stripe in a group of three hillocks, each time
flanked by the reds above and below. Yes, and in every
case, there was a gray-tan layer beneath the red. As far
as he could distinguish color, the patterns repeated.
Aiee, this was indeed a sacred place!

Hunger pangs distracted him, and he took a sip of
water and then continued to walk slowly and observe
the ever-changing colors of the canyon. The day
passed for him more quickly than one might think.

Afternoon shadows began to grow in the gorge, lengthening and stretching to crawl across the canyon floor, across the backs of the shifting herd, and up the colorfully striped cones and spires. Just before Sun Boy slipped beyond earth's rim, the canyon seemed bathed in a golden glow, changing to purple shadow as day faded.

The slender slice of the new moon, a little thicker and lagging a little farther behind Sun, hung in the west over the canyon. Below, the herd rested quietly, softly muttering, shifting comfortably in the deepening darkness.

17

>> >> >>

He saddled the stallion as soon as it was light. On the previous day he had chosen the trail that he would take down the cliff's face. It was plain to see that the buffalo had been using these obscure paths, and it required only that he choose one that appeared well worn. He was alert, with the increased clarity that resulted from the fast. There was an intensified use of all his senses. Hearing, vision, smell—all were more acute as he moved into this important phase of his mission.

He wondered about the whereabouts of Digging Owl. He had spent some time last evening, looking for a sign of Owl's night fire, but he saw nothing. He had been puzzled, because he should have been able to see any camp within a day's travel—at least, any camp on the upper plateau. It was possible, of course, that Digging Owl had descended into the canyon already and that his fire had been hidden by the uneven terrain, or by the irregularities of the bluff's face. Yes, Horse thought, a fire just at the base of the cliff wall, but at a little distance, would be out of sight. There might even be caves in the wall. Well, no matter. Except he wished that he knew what Owl intended to do.

He had also spent some time looking for the distant point of light he had seen before. There had been only darkness, and he wondered if his senses had been deceiving him. Had he *really* seen a light that might have been a distant campfire?

Now he considered his descent into the canyon. He could give the horse his head and rely on the sure-footed animal to carry him safely. However, the trails were made and used by animals—buffalo, deer, possibly elk and antelope, maybe even wild horses. He had no way of knowing if they were wide enough for a man on horseback. If there was no space for a knee alongside the horse's shoulder, and a steep drop on the other side . . . he had no desire to test the result. His was the prairie country anyway, not that of cliffs and narrow trails. In the end he decided to walk down, leading the stallion.

It was an easy descent, only one or two steep places. He thought perhaps he could ride on the way back up, if he happened to use this same trail. He marked it in his mind, as he mounted the roan, by three brightly striped hillocks near the lower end. Yes, he could find this path again.

The stallion was quieter now, having decided that this was *not* a buffalo hunt—at least, not yet. The grazing buffalo, in turn, were quiet, unimpressed by the horse and rider who moved among them. The nearer animals raised their heads to stare curiously. It was apparent that they had not been hunted—at least, not recently. One massive old bull shook his head threat-eningly and pawed the ground, throwing up chunks of sod. Red Horse carefully reined aside, still at a walk, and moved around the bull at a safe distance.

He started in a southwesterly direction, following what seemed to be the direction of the canyon's shape. The steep cliff was at his right, rising in a red and yellow wall to end in a sharp edge at the top against blue sky. It was hard to estimate the height, looking almost straight up in this way. How high would an arrow reach, launched upward against the cliff? He was sure it could go no more than halfway. And on the level, a good bowman might drive an arrow well over a hundred paces. *Aiee,* the size was deceptive!

As if to verify this impression, he came upon an old giant of a cottonwood tree, growing closely against the cliff's base, yet it was dwarfed by the wall above.

But while these observations were interesting, even exciting, the size of the canyon was not of primary importance. Except, of course, that it was large enough to have furnished a haven for this immense herd of buffalo. He could see now that they spread on out to the southwest, as far as the eye could see.

He was unsure what he was supposed to do now. Surely he should have some sort of a plan, instead of merely wandering aimlessly. He stopped and dis-mounted to let the stallion graze a little, while he thought it over. His ultimate goal, he was certain, was to find the white bull. But how? He had felt on the previous day that the search was much like sorting grains of sand to find one of the proper color. He was even more convinced today. He had seen thousands of buffalo, but not the white bull that he sought. What other way to search might there be? A doubt flickered in the back of his mind. Maybe the main purpose of his quest, like that of Digging Owl, was simply to induce the herd to leave the canyon and move northward. But if so, why had he been shown the white bull? And Owl's medicine had suggested to him that the two *not* work together.

Red Horse sighed deeply. He was being too impatient, he knew. When the time was right, when *he* was ready, he would be shown what he must do. Meanwhile . . . well, why was he riding the valley floor? It had been suggested by the appearance of his spirit-guide. When any change was required, surely he would be shown—if he was receptive, of course. That had always been a difficult thing, his tendency to try too hard, to want to push too fast. It had been difficult for him to be patient enough to accept the spirit-gifts of an apprentice holy man as they came. He could always recognize when he had pushed too hard, been too impatient, but only afterward. He must go slowly and watch for signs. He remounted and rode on, still at a careful walk, to avoid alarming the buffalo. Later, he would consider killing one for food. His supplies were short, but just now he was fasting and in no need. Maybe in a day or two . . . surely he would have some sort of sign by that time.

He camped for the night in a little pocket against the base of the cliff, where a spring trickled forth. Someone long ago had placed stones to contain a pool of the spring water. The pool was sheltered by the rocky overhang, which also prevented trampling by the buffalo or other animals. He drank deeply, grateful for the efforts of the unknown benefactor who had placed the stones. This was the first sign of human habitation he had encountered here, and it seemed very old. Some of the stones were entwined in the roots of a tree of considerable size.

He built his night fire against the wall, noticing as he did so that someone, maybe generations before, had done the same. On the overhang above his head was a smudge of long-cold smoke. Silently, he sent out a thought to whatever spirits of the Old Ones might still inhabit here and asked their approval for his mission. He sat by his little fire of cottonwood sticks, studying the shifting patterns of the red embers, the dreams and pictures they suggested. Finally he rolled in his robe and slept. His last thought before he fell asleep was that tomorrow must be a day that was a turning point. Not merely in his own life, but in the history of the People.

Red Horse awoke, surprised that it was nearing dawn. He had expected to have visions and dreams, to experience meaningful things that would help to bring meaning to the confusion of this entire quest. But there had been nothing. He had merely slept.

He wondered about the whereabouts of Digging Owl, and whether Owl had identified *his* mission and how it was to be carried out. Horse felt that he was no nearer to understanding what he must do next than when he started.

He performed the Morning Song to greet the day. It would be some time before Sun rose high enough above the canyon for the rays to reach his camp, but it was growing light now. He found himself in no hurry to start on. Maybe it was because of the frustration he had encountered in searching thousands of animals for one elusive white bull. Or possibly he was feeling a certain contentment here at this campsite, the contentment, perhaps, that had been felt by that ancient traveler who had built the fire whose smoke had blackened the overhang. Maybe he was feeling the spirit of the man who had dug out the little basin for the spring and had placed the stones with care. It was quite possible that this had been a place of habitation, not just a stopover. It would be a good place to winter, he thought, sheltered from the northwest winds.

He wandered a few steps along the canyon wall. Yes, in the better light of day, he could see more smoke-blackened spots. This had been a place where many had camped or lived, maybe since Creation. He felt no urgency to leave and continue his search. Finally it came to him: he should wait here, for whatever was to come next! Yes, that must be it. He rebuilt his fire, to indicate to the spirits that he would stay, and then went to picket the stallion in a place with a new supply of grass.

A few paces away, a large rock, squarish in shape and taller than a man, had fallen from the cliff, probably ages ago. It seemed to present a good lookout, so he climbed to the top to view the valley and the slowly milling buffalo as they grazed or rested. Maybe this was intended—that he watch from here as the buffalo passed, singly, in twos and threes, or in larger bands. Maybe the white bull would come to him.

He knew this was wishful thinking, but it was attractive. It was much easier to sit on a rock in the warm sun than to ride aimlessly through the herd. Even with as comfortable a horse as the roan stallion, it would be tiring. The thing that finally decided him was the horse. It would be good to let the roan have some time to eat and recover the weight lost in the arduous trip through the desert plains.

By midday the sun was so hot that the rock was uncomfortable. However, the cottonwood tree now presented some shade, and he changed his position to take advantage of it. He had seen innumerable buffalo, some in varying shades of brown and tan, but no sign of the white bull.

How long should he fast? There must be a point at which he would become weak, too weak to hunt when the time came. But before then, there should be some sort of vision . . . or at least a sign. The time of hunger pangs had passed; his thinking was clear and he could wait.

It was late afternoon, with the shadows of the canyon walls beginning to creep across the floor, when he heard the sound. It was a rhythmic beat, a clicking rattle that he first mistook for the murmur of the cottonwood leaves overhead. He was puzzled by the rhythm for a moment, but then he realized that the sound came from the top of the cliff, perhaps a bow shot to his left. It was a little longer before he realized that there was a singsong chanting, too, rising and falling on the wind.

It did not take long to know that this was a ceremonial dance and song. He could not see the singer from his position on the rock, but he thought he recognized the voice and the rhythm. This must be Digging Owl, and this was the time that Owl had been led to initiate his medicine. But what? What was Owl's purpose, and what could be expected to happen now?

18

>> >> >>

As he listened, Red Horse attempted to decide what sort of ceremony Owl was performing. What was the holy man trying to accomplish? It seemed certain that his ultimate goal was to bring the errant buffalo herd up and out of the canyon and start them northward. Just how Digging Owl intended to accomplish this was a mystery. However, it must have something to do with the ceremony that was now going on at the rim above.

He climbed down from his observation post and moved a few steps out into the open, away from the wall, to try to see the dancer. There was a snort behind him, and he turned to see a young bull, only a stone's throw away. The bull was apparently offended by the unfamiliar sight of a man on foot and was ready to challenge him. The animal tossed his massive head, muttering and pawing the sod, tossing chunks of dirt and grass over his back with horns and hooves.

Fighting panic, Red Horse carefully turned his head to look toward the canyon wall. There lay the safety of broken rocks, boulders, trees, and brush. But he did not think there was time . . . no, surely the bull would be upon him before he reached the wall. He could not run.

During his apprenticeship, he had learned the skills of buffalo medicine and how to work with the calfskin cape. The calfskin was, in fact, carefully rolled and in his pack, over near the fire. He had brought it on this journey, because of the nature of the quest. The skills of working with the buffalo were seldom used now, since the hunt was easier with the horse. But the methods had been passed down through the generations, from one holy man to the next. Red Horse had paid his time, moving through a herd, with the skin tied over him, disguised as a young calf. It had taken a great deal of courage the first few times, knowing that the shiny black horns of any one of the great creatures could disembowel him in an instant.

The most important lesson to be learned by this instruction and practice, however, had been that of the spirit. It was necessary not only to act like a buffalo but to think like one, to get inside the head of the animal.

Now here he was, defenseless, in the open, and vulnerable to an aggressive young bull. And he did not even have the calfskin. He steadied himself and tried to ignore the fear that clutched at his stomach. He must not show fear; even the smell of fear might loose the charge. He thought quickly but carefully, letting his spirit reach out toward the bull even as he did so.

Peace, my brother, his thoughts said silently. *I mean you no harm.*

It was good that Red Horse was in the fasting state,

for it helped clarify things of the spirit. He felt the momentary confusion in the thoughts of the bull. But it was not enough. If the animal came to a decision, it would be on the side of aggression. Maybe he could take advantage of the confusion. The animal was still trying to determine the nature of this strange creature; probably the unfamiliar two-legged gait had caught the bull's attention from the first. And the way to safety for a holy man's apprentice in a calfskin was to act like a calf, to move like one. Many times he had playfully butted and frolicked with a real buffalo calf, while the older animals grazed only an arm's length away. As a young man, he had enjoyed the danger, though his father had disapproved of the risks he took.

But now he could not readily assume the posture and motion of a calf, especially without the cape for disguise. However, a man, moving directly away, might appear calflike—especially with the buffalo's poor eyesight. All of this was racing through his head in the space of a few heartbeats as he turned deliberately and started to move away. He tried to project a comfortable, dull spirit toward the bull, a grazing, slow-moving herd-spirit. He dared not doubt that this would work. Each step was carefully calculated—by its length and cadence, the sway of his body—to appear to the bull like another buffalo, walking directly away. Careful, now: three or four steps, pause, bend a little to appear to graze, another step. He could feel the bull begin to relax, though still a bit puzzled. The animal did not quite understand this strange creature, which now appeared to be a buffalo. There was a moment when Red Horse feared that the bull would even yet approach to investigate. He tried to put that thought out of his mind, lest he suggest it to the bull.

He swung his head and left shoulder irritably, as if ridding himself of a biting fly.

Apparently that motion convinced the bull. Horse dared not look, but he felt the animal relax, and he knew when it lowered its head to resume grazing. Now that he had reached the safety of the broken rocks, he paused a moment to relax. He must be more careful. That had been a stupid error.

Above him on the cliff, the cadence of the chant still sounded. He had not been able to catch a glimpse of Digging Owl, and it seemed certain that he could not, from here. And as he had already discovered, it seemed inadvisable to venture out into the open away from the canyon wall. Yet he felt that he must at least see what Digging Owl was doing. He did not relish the idea of a climb up the cliff's face and down again, but there seemed no other way.

He checked to make certain that the stallion was picketed securely and stowed his packs and saddle beneath the overhang. Then he began to look for the likeliest trail to the top.

It did not take long, because he had already taken care to note where the paths in the immediate area began the climb. Now he selected the one that showed the greatest amount of wear and started upward. The going was not hard, though he soon found himself breathing heavily from the exertion. It was much easier, he reflected, coming down. He reached the top, rising cautiously at first until he could see what he might encounter.

Digging Owl, a bow shot away, was dancing and chanting near the canyon's rim. Red Horse, with the practiced eye of a medicine man, saw immediately that Owl's body paint design was the same that he had worn before. This ceremony, then, was quite likely the same. The cadence and the song, though Horse did not know the tongue, seemed the same or remarkably similar.

A rain dance? thought Red Horse, puzzled. He looked across the floor of the canyon, and the vast herd that extended to the plain beyond. Slowly, he began to understand. A rain would come from the southwest, causing the herd to drift away from it to the northeast. They would move up and out and onto the plain above, to resume more normal migration. This was to be Digging Owl's medicine, then, his manner of getting the herd moving up and out of the "hole."

Horse must not disturb or interrupt the ceremony. It would be to interfere in another's medicine. He sat down, waiting quietly, watching the dance. He did not know whether Digging Owl saw him or not and did not particularly care. Owl knew that he was in the area and that both sought the answer to the same problem. He would not intrude, but he felt that for his own safety he should know what was happening.

The herd was becoming restless at some unseen change, some shift in the light breeze. In the far distance, to the southwest, Horse sensed, rather than saw, the heavier blue line that signaled a storm front. He even thought he could sense the distant mutter of Rain Maker's drum, though it may have been only the mutter of the restless herd.

It was not long, however, until he was certain. He could see the fluttering orange glow in the advancing cloud. An alarming thought struck him. When Rain Makes arrived here, throwing his spears of real-fire, it was no time to be in the open, at the top of the cliff. He would wait only a little longer . . . no! He must go now! Soon the buffalo would be moving, starting to crowd their way up the trails to the top, and he would find no path on which to retreat. He turned and started down, as rapidly as he could in the gathering darkness.

Above him, the rain song of Digging Owl continued in rising and falling cadence. Owl must retreat soon too, he thought. But then the truth sank home. Digging Owl had no intention of retreating. The holy man had totally dedicated himself to this, his main purpose, the bringing back of the buffalo.

By the time Red Horse reached the lower portion of the trail, he could begin to distinguish individual drum rolls of thunder and could see distant flashes of real-fire as the spears stabbed at the earth. An old cow blocked the trail, and he fitted an arrow to his bow string, prepared to stop her if he must. At the last moment the animal whirled, pushing others aside in her retreat. Red Horse hurried down the trail behind her, thankful for the cow's help in clearing his path. He could see other animals on other paths, starting to climb toward the top, up and out of the canyon, retreating from the storm.

It was darkening when he reached the canyon floor and sprinted toward his campsite. He must somehow avoid the crushing mass of the herd. . . . Dodging, twisting, he managed to reach the rock where he had spent the day.

There was a boom of thunder, nearer now, followed by a steady rumble to the southwest. The herd was beginning to run. He climbed the rock, barely before the crushing mass swept past him, like the rolling waters of a flash flood. He caught a glimpse of the stallion, apparently broken loose and running with the stampede. He saw a yearling lose its footing and fall, to be pounded into the dirt by a hundred hooves. Dust rolled up, choking him. He was dimly aware of the rhythmic chant above, barely heard now above the earth-shaking thunder around him.

Then the rain swept in, a pelting, driving rain that almost instantly settled the dust. He sat up, breathing more easily but now unable to see beyond the driving curtain and the rush of the closest of the dark bodies.

A deafening crack, with a simultaneous blinding flash of real-fire, told him that Rain Maker's target had been the cliff above. He glanced upward. In a flicker of light, he caught a glimpse of a falling object, which disappeared into the swirling dark mass only a few steps in front of him. Digging Owl had asked the ultimate of his medicine and had offered his life in exchange.

Red Horse realized in that instant that Owl had probably been totally aware and had even planned it this way. He had insisted that they separate . . . of course! For the safety of his companion. Horse stared, not seeing. He wished he could have spoken to Digging Owl before . . . could have told him that he understood, that he respected. . . .

There was another flash. Not the booming, blinding crash but a flicker of illumination for a moment. Red Horse gasped. There, only a stone's throw away, stood the white bull of his vision. It was standing on a little hillock, above the herd. The animals seemed to be dividing, sliding around the hillock like water around a stone in the stream. Then it was dark again, and there was only the driving rain and the sound of the rushing herd below his rock.

19

>> >> >>

Horse lay shivering on the rock, the cold rain
pelting down, elated, yet awed. It had been so sudden
and gone so quickly. The picture of the white bull,
standing majestically on the hillock, was burned into
his mind. Was it only a vision? No, he was sure it had
been real. A thing of the spirit, yet real flesh and blood.
He watched in the darkness for the next flicker of
light. When it came, he was disappointed. There was
nothing. He could make out the hillock where the bull
had stood, but only by the flow of running animals
moving over it. The appearance was that of a swell in
the surface of a moving stream. But there was no trace
of the white bull.

He began to doubt his senses. Could he have been
mistaken? Was it a trick, an illusion caused by light and
shadow and gusts of driving rain? Though he was
tuned to things of illusion in his profession as holy
man, he could not make himself believe so. He had

plainly seen the bull, the majesty of the creature, and the flow of the herd around it. Well, no matter. He must wait for daylight now. He settled into the most comfortable position that the rock afforded. It was a matter of degree. Not comfortable but less *un*comfortable, perhaps.

He had sheltered his bow under his body as best he could, to keep it from the sluggishness of action that he knew would result from wetting the wood and the bow string. Already he was planning his moves for the coming day. The storm should be over soon. The sound of Rain Maker's drum was receding into the distance. The sun would quickly warm and dry his garments and his weapon, but his problems might be just beginning. He was certain that Digging Owl had been killed by the real-fire. If not, surely by the fall from the cliff or by the trampling stampede. It was doubtful whether there would even be enough flesh and bone left to identify, after a thousand hooves had pounded the body into the canyon floor. Again, Horse thought with respect and admiration of the holy man who had become his friend for a little while. Owl must have planned his final dance ceremony well in advance, a self-sacrifice for his people and for all of those whose lives depended on the return of the buffalo. From the Other Side, Digging Owl must look back with pride on his final plunge from the cliff.

Red Horse shook his head to clear it of such thoughts. He managed to sleep a little at intervals, and each time was wakened by exciting glimpses of the white bull. The meaning must be good, he thought. At least, it verified his impression that this was his mission. He must also begin to consider when his fast should be ended. He would eventually become weak. Well, he would look for a sign.

Above all, however, he was concerned over the loss of his horse. He had caught a single glimpse of the roan after it had broken loose from the tether and was being swept away with the herd. He could survive, of course, without it, but it would not be easy. He had counted on the animal's skill to help him bring down the white bull. But beyond that, how was he to get home? Even if his quest for the bull was successful, what then? He dreaded the long dry trek across the desert plains. In addition, he hoped to be carrying the heavy skin of the bull. Maybe he could find another horse. Digging Owl's horse might even still be in the area.

The night seemed endless, though the storm did pass, and the stars came out to glitter reassuringly overhead. Horse was glad when he could detect the change from black to yellow-gray in the east as dawn approached. Eagerly, he waited to see what daylight would reveal. Very gradually, he could make out the occasional carcass of a buffalo, trampled in the stampede and pounded into a shapeless mass. Coyotes were moving, searching for an easy meal. He saw another movement, nearer the wall, and identified a young cow, limping on a crippled leg. There must be other injured animals. Surely he would have no trouble obtaining meat, even on foot, when the time came.

As the light became stronger, he tried to see where Digging Owl might have fallen. He could not be sure —he had seen the fall only by a flash of real-fire—but he surveyed the general area from his vantage point on the rock. The spot where Owl's falling form would have come to rest was now a watercourse. Yes, he remembered, there had been a dry depression, a wet-weather stream bed, now a receding current after the rain. Anything that remained of Owl's body in the stampede would have been carried away in the flash-flooding torrent.

There seemed no point in a search. It was the way of things. Owl's body had been nourished on the flesh of the buffalo, who in turn had been nourished by the grass. In dying as he had, Digging Owl had returned to the earth, to nourish the growth of next year's grass and begin the ancient cycle again. Owl had wished it so, and Red Horse could want no more fitting tribute for his friend. Solemnly, he raised his face to the sky and lifted his voice in the Song of Mourning of the People.

It was fully daylight now, the sun peeping over the distant horizon but not yet reaching the canyon with its rays. Red Horse began to see that there were still scattered groups of buffalo, left behind by the departure of the main herd. Now he faced a new problem. Should he leave the canyon to seek the white bull? The vast majority of the buffalo had gone, and it seemed likely that the bull had stayed with the main herd.

Yet he was reluctant to leave the canyon. His medicine, his visions, had brought him to this place. Part of the purpose of his quest had been fulfilled. The buffalo had returned up and out of the Hole-in-the-Earth, as Digging Owl had called it. But he, Red Horse, had not had any part in that. He had been only an observer. So there must be more to his having been guided here. He needed a further sign, a guidance as to how he must proceed. Meanwhile, as he waited, he would search on foot for the roan stallion.

He descended from the rock and stood for a moment, looking up and down the canyon. He paused to test his bowstring, plucking it with his thumb. The twang was muffled, indicating that the twisted gut was still damp. But it was drying, and even now it was usable in an emergency. The wood itself had not absorbed much rain, being heavily coated with tallow to shed water.

Horse moved upstream, for no particular reason except that the brush and small trees were more numerous there. He might as well investigate that thicket near at hand, before moving on. There was a slight movement in the brush, and a half-grown calf burst into the open, startling him. He had half lifted his bow by pure reflex before he identified the animal. He moved into the fringe of willows, perhaps a stone's throw in length and a few paces in width. It was the sort of place that a horse might hide, and near the area where he had last seen the stallion. He peered cautiously ahead. Yes, there was a motion; a light-colored animal stood in the mottled shade of the willows, well hidden by the shifting light and shade of the thicket. Another movement, like a tossing of the head by an animal that fights the clinging deerflies. Good. He was feeling better, more confident as he lowered the bow and stepped forward to retrieve the stallion.

Horse moved quietly, because the roan might still be skittish from the excitement of the storm. In his hand he carried a rawhide thong, to fashion a bridle when he had reached the animal. He peered through the last thin screen of willows and gasped in amazement. The animal that stood there in the mottled shade that now proved so deceiving was not the roan stallion but a magnificent white buffalo. It seemed unaware of his presence. Enthralled, he stared at the creature.

Probably no more than five summers of age, the bull was at the physical peak of its strength and agility. The great head tossed again, brushing flies from the creamy back. Red Horse did not see how the animal could appear so clean, after the dusty encounter of last night. The rain, maybe. He was close enough to see every detail of the animal's appearance, even the tiny bead of fresh blood on the tender skin of the nose, where a fly had bitten. The eyes were red, as they had been in his vision. The thought crossed his mind that the bright sunlight must be painful to such eyes. This explained the bull's tendency to hide in the shade during the brightness of day. Also, possibly, why white buffalo, though known to exist, were seldom seen. They must seek the shade and move into the open only in darkness.

Even as these thoughts bounded through his brain, he was fitting an arrow to his string. He was trembling, and his hands were damp. He must not miss; the future of the People depended on it. He considered where he should aim. A heart shot? No, an animal struck there, even though surely dying, would often run wildly, and could cover some distance while the hunter pursued on foot. A lung shot? Yes, that would be slower, but not so likely to cause a panicky run. He lifted the bow and concentrated on the area behind the front leg. A little farther back . . . the string twanged and the arrow leaped forward. He saw the bull flinch slightly as the shaft disappeared to the feathers between the ribs. The great head tossed, as if to brush off the annoying biting insect that had jabbed its ribs.

The animal stood, appearing confused, and a trickle of blood appeared at the nostrils. It took a few steps and then lay down, slowly and ponderously, as if to rest. The breathing became heavier and then was still. The little red eyes lost the light that told of life.

Red Horse stepped from concealment and approached the bull, shaking with excitement and awe.

"My brother, I am sorry to kill you," he recited sincerely, *"but the future of my people depends upon it."*

He finished the apology and moved forward to examine the prize. The white coat was thick and rich, in excellent condition considering the season. There was none of the ragged, matted fur, partly shed for the summer, so often seen at this time. Now he must plan the skinning and treatment of the pelt. He studied the position of the bull, lying on its side. He could make the necessary cuts in the skin without effort and skin the upper side. But he must find a way to roll the carcass over. The usual way was with the help of a horse. Delay would be a catastrophe also. Unless the skin was separated from the warm body in a reasonably short time, the hair would start to fall out. Maybe he could roll the animal with the help of a pry, the use of a pole to assist. Barring that, he would have to cut the carcass apart to drag the skin free. There was no time to lose.

He cut the throat, to allow it to bleed, and made the incisions in the belly skin and in the inside of each leg. The bull was fat, he noticed as he began to work the skin loose. He could break his fast, now, and he began to think of the mouth-watering goodness of broiling hump ribs over a fire. It should be the best of medicines to end his fast with the flesh of this most powerful of medicine-creatures. But first he must finish the skinning, in one way or another, and allow the hide to cool.

His attention was so preoccupied with the task that he did not hear the approach of the horses until they were within a few paces. Then he heard the muffled clump of hooves in the sand and looked up. He was hoping that his own horse had wandered back, though that was a slim possibility at best. In truth, the roan was one of the horses that he saw, but it was being led on a rope by one of the riders. The men were strangers, with garments and equipment like none he had seen before. He was reminded of his first meeting with Digging Owl, except that these three men showed even more hostility than the bowlegged leader of Owl's party.

The heart of Red Horse was very heavy as he straightened and turned to face this new threat to his quest.

20
>> >> >>

As the warriors approached, Red Horse thought of the twinkling fire he had seen in the distance, on their first night at the canyon. He had not had occasion to wonder about it. But it was a logical thing that in so favorable a country there would be those who lived and hunted here.

He had only a few moments to think about how he would try to deal with this confrontation. He must, for the sake of his nation, handle it successfully. His medicine had brought him this far, but, powerful though it might be, it could be overcome. If, for instance, one of the warriors behaved on impulse, Red Horse could be dead within the space of a few heartbeats. Then his medicine would mean nothing.

He decided to try to act as if this meeting was out of the ordinary only in that his kill was a very special medicine-animal.

"Ah-koh!" he greeted aloud, at the same time giving the hand-sign greeting.

The three drew their horses to a stop but did not reply. Two of the men were talking excitedly, pointing at the half-skinned white bull. Could it be, he wondered, that these people did not use hand signs?

"Do you speak with the signs?" he asked.

It seemed a long time before the man in the middle nodded, with a grunt that may have been an affirmative. Red Horse felt that he must push on, to keep the initiative in this conversation that seemed one-sided so far.

"I am pleased to see you," he signed. "Thank you for returning my horse."

A grumbling remark passed among the three.

"We will share some of the meat of my medicine-kill," he offered, "but I need the horse to roll it over and free the skin."

The three sat on their horses and said nothing. Horse began to wonder whether they actually did know the hand signs.

"How are you called?" he asked.

"That is no matter to you," the leader signed. "And this is our horse. We found him. Who are you, and why do you hunt in the country of our nation?"

"I am called Red Horse. I am a holy man, from far away, on a vision-quest for this bull."

"For *this* bull?"

"Yes. I saw him in a vision and was sent to find the white cape. Come, let me finish the skinning, before it begins to spoil."

Boldly, he walked to the roan and started to take the lead rope. He stopped suddenly as he was confronted with a wicked-looking lance, pointed at his throat in a very convincing manner. Well, he decided, he could not back down now. He stood his ground, and began to sign again, trying not to show the near panic that he felt.

"Look," he stated with the hand signs, "this medicine-skin will spoil while we argue. Let me turn the bull and finish skinning. We can argue while the skin cools and our meat cooks."

The man with the spear hesitated, but the other two were nodding. With this encouragement, Red Horse carefully pushed the spear aside, even while he dreaded the other's reaction. He took the stallion's rope and led him into position to accomplish the pull. The warriors were dismounting.

"There is water there, by the tree." He pointed to the spring under the rock.

Two of the men walked over to drink, and the third stayed to watch him. He was gaining time while he carried out the necessary task of completing the skinning. But he was also gaining confidence. These men must be impressed with the power of the medicine of one who could follow a vision to find a sacred animal far away. They were still distrustful, however. It was entirely possible that they would covet the white buffalo cape enough to kill him and take it. They might even kill him just for the horse. He must continue as if he had all the confidence in the world in the knowledge of his medicine's strength.

The two men returned, and the third went to the spring.

"Build a fire," Red Horse signed. "We will have meat."

The half-skinned carcass tilted, legs in the air, and dropped ponderously to the already-skinned side, as the roan leaned into the ropes. Red Horse untied and released the roan to forage with the other horses, while he returned to finish the task of skinning.

By common consent, it seemed, any argument was deferred until after the meat was cooked. Red Horse realized that it was good to postpone any confrontation, or even discussion, as long as possible. He spread the white pelt over a bush to cool and turned back to the carcass. The very best of the hump ribs . . . he removed and propped the ribs over the fire, with the help of the man who had kindled it. Horse cut a small piece of the choicest meat and sacrificed it in the fire, with a brief prayer to the spirits of the canyon.

Finally, when everyone had eaten his fill of well-browned ribs and even the bones themselves were gnawed, the conversation could be delayed no longer. While they ate, they had discussed such things as the weather and the strange behavior of the buffalo this past season. The odd, fast-moving storm was mentioned, as it had moved the herd up and out of the canyon. This seemed not to be regarded as especially undesirable by these natives of the area. They were accustomed to the presence of the herds only for the winter season anyway. Some of the animals usually remained for the summer, they indicated. It was good that the herd appeared now to be ready to resume the normal migration.

"Did you bring the storm?" one man asked directly.

"No. There was another . . . a holy man of another nation. It was his dance ceremony."

"Yes, we saw his fire. Or yours, maybe. Where is he now?"

"Dead."

Horse described the real-fire, and Digging Owl's plunge from the cliff top.

"Then where is his body?" asked the leader suspiciously. "And if his medicine was so powerful, why is he dead?"

"Ah, my friends, I do not know all things," Red Horse signed seriously. "But I am made to think that he gave his life for this, to move the buffalo."

"As you would give yours for this white cape?"

There was an ominous undertone here that Horse did not like. Here, then, came the confrontation.

"I would have," he signed. "Of course, I must now tan the cape and take it back to my people. And I thank you for helping me by returning my horse."

The dour-faced leader chuckled, but with little humor. "We will give you the horse," he signed, "but the white skin is ours."

Red Horse felt his stomach tighten like a fist. He tried to retain his composure.

"My friend, that cannot be," Horse signed. "My vision . . . I have been called to this. The white buffalo, the cape—"

"That is no worry of ours," signed the other. "We could kill you and take both horse and cape."

"No!" Red Horse indicated firmly. He was surprised at himself, but he was losing his fear in the intensity of the moment. He had not come this far, suffered this much, to give up the most important deed of his life. "The cape is not yours, my friends. It is not even mine. It is a thing of medicine, the medicine of my people."

The leader jerked a knife from his waist, pointing it directly at Red Horse.

"Is your medicine stronger than this?" he demanded.

Red Horse noticed that the other two men appeared confused. They whispered together and seemed to be concerned over their leader's actions. Horse managed a chuckle.

"Of course," he indicated, hoping to appear as confident as he sounded. "My gift has brought me across the desert, all the way from the Sacred Hills, to this white bull. How can you deny it?"

The other man sat, glaring. There was a shadow of doubt in his face. This was the dangerous point. Horse tried to ready himself, in case he was attacked. He feared he would be no match for the wiry warrior, but he must do his best to survive, for the good of the People.

"Take the cape," the warrior said finally, "but I keep the horse."

Red Horse considered this possibility. It was a compromise that might work. At least, it would get him out alive. But he thought again. What use to leave here alive, only to die in the desert? He could not cross that sandy waste on foot, carrying packs as well as the heavy white skin. He shook his head.

"My brother does not understand," he indicated charitably. "The horse is part of the medicine." He touched the bit that dangled from his neck on its thong. "This, too, is part of it. It allows my nation to control the horse."

"Then I will take it too," suggested the other.

Maybe he had gone too far, Red Horse thought to himself. If he were killed, not only would the cape be lost, and Long Lance's horse, but the elk-dog medicine. *Aiee,* maybe this was a mistake.

"Let me show you," he signed confidently.

He rose and went to where the roan stallion was grazing. He was thinking rapidly, trying to conceive a way to impress the doubter. What better way than to use the talisman itself? The bit had not been in the mouth of a horse for generations, probably, but was said to give complete control. He devoutly hoped so.

He took the bit from his neck and untied the thong, retying it in the position of use. At least, he hoped so. He had never actually seen it used in a horse's mouth. It seemed to fit well. The roan rolled his tongue on the unfamiliar object but appeared to understand it. Red Horse swung to the animal's back. He was delighted at the responsiveness of the roan. First, he paraded through the horse's gaits. Walk, trot, lope, and fast sprint. It took a very light hand on the thongs that served as reins. He could see that the watching men were impressed.

Then he reined in toward the fire and motioned them to hand him his bow and arrows. One of the men did so. A mock charge, an arrow into the carcass of the bull. Wheel, circle, another. Three arrows in all, into a spot that could be covered with the palm of a man's hand. Then he wheeled back toward the fire and brought the roan to a sliding stop. He stepped to the ground, stripped the bit from the stallion's mouth, and turned to the waiting men.

Two of the warriors stood in open-mouthed awe, as Horse retied the thongs and hung the bit once more on his chest. Only the third man seemed unconvinced.

"It is nothing," he signed. "A good horse, a skilled horseman. I could do the same."

"Of course," Red Horse agreed, "but that is the point. I am *not* a skilled horseman, but only a holy man whose medicine can make these things happen."

The other man shook his head. "That is not good enough. Show us your medicine."

This was an unreasonable demand, and the other two knew it. One does not exhibit the strength of his medicine for such a demand. It was insulting, and an invasion of the holy man's privacy. One of the warriors started to protest, but Red Horse silenced him with a wave of the hand.

"My friend," he signed to the unconvinced one, "your request is very rude, but my medicine is strong enough to honor it. I will show you, and then I have a plan to propose."

There was nothing but a shrug and a grunt from the other, so Horse turned to his medicine bag. He had brought with him, for no special reason at the time, the Black Stones. Handed down through generations of holy men, the plum stones were said to represent very powerful medicine. They were quite similar to the plum stones used in the gambling games. One side of each seed was of the natural yellow color, and on the other side was placed a red dot. Gamblers would roll an odd number of plum stones, placing bets on red or yellow.

The Black Stones, however, held special significance. Instead of a red dot, one entire side of each plum stone was painted black. They were nine in number. Their secret, handed down with the stones from one holy man to another, was simple. These plum seeds were specially selected. Each was slightly flatter on the unpainted side. Thus the odds were weighted. There would be a majority of black showing at every toss.

He spread his sleeping robe, skin side up, on a flat area and took the little rawhide case out of his medicine bag.

"Now," he explained, "I will roll nine stones. Each is black on one side, yellow on the other. I will ask the stones whether your wish for the cape is good. If it is, the stones will show the yellow color of the sun. If not, they will be black."

Red Horse rattled the container and tossed the contents across the surface of the robe. The plum stones skittered and jumped convincingly and came to rest . . . five black, four yellow.

"Again!" motioned the suspicious one.

Horse gathered the seeds and returned them to the container, to toss again. This time there were seven black, two yellow.

"It is a trick," the other man signed.

Red Horse shook his head in denial and picked up the plum stones again, placing them in the box.

"You try it," he offered.

The untrusting warrior was suspicious, but he took the container and rolled the seeds out on the surface of the skin. They tumbled to rest with eight showing black, only one yellow. There were gasps from the other two men. Even Red Horse was surprised, though he tried not to show it.

"It is as I said," he signed quickly, gathering the plum stones before anyone began to examine them. "You can see the power of my medicine. Now, my proposal: I take the cape of my people and the horse. I give you the meat of the sacred kill, all but the brain and part of the liver, which I need to tan the cape. I need the horns, too, but the rest is yours. One other thing. Because of our friendship—after all, we have eaten together—because of this, I give you the skin of the seed sac, the scrotum of the bull, for a medicine bag."

Again, the two lesser warriors gasped at such generosity, but the reluctant one was silent a long time. Finally, he took a long breath.

"And if I kill you anyway?"

Red Horse now felt that he was winning, and it was an exhilarating feeling. He looked the other man straight in the eye.

"Do you want to take the risk?"

The moments passed, but finally the man shook his head.

"No," he signed. "It is good, as you say it."

21

>> >> >>

They worked together, butchering out the best portions of the meat, preparing some to dry. Red Horse would be here for several days, for the proper curing of the white cape. It would be only sensible to have strips of meat drying at the same time, to provide supplies for his journey home.

The others were quite agreeable in this, as there was much more meat than they could transport anyway. Their village was a day's journey to the south. They decided simply to trim out all the meat they could carry, of the choicest cuts, and take it home to finish the stripping and drying. By the time this was accomplished, shadows were long, and they decided to camp for the night, to make their trip tomorrow.

The evening offered opportunity for relaxation, eating, and exchange of stories. The Creation story of the strangers, who called themselves Hasanai, was one that Red Horse had never heard before. They, like the People, had come from the inside of the earth.

"The first one out was an old man," the storyteller related. "In one hand he carried a drum and, in the other, fire and a medicine pipe."

Red Horse nodded, and the other continued.

"The second person was a woman, the Mother of the Hasanai, the People. She carried seeds of corn and pumpkins."

"Your people are Growers?" Red Horse asked.

"Yes, since the First Ones. But we also hunt."

"What is the meaning of Hasanai?" he asked.

"It is 'Our People.' Is not yours the same?"

"Yes . . . everyone's name for themselves, maybe," Red Horse agreed. "Others sometimes call us 'Elk-dog People.' "

The others nodded in understanding.

"Are all your horses like this one?"

"Mostly," signed Red Horse, boasting a little. "This one is special. He has the blood of two great horses. One, a gray mare, called the First Elk-dog, wore this medicine bit. The other, much later, is the Dream Horse, sometimes called Fire Horse, because of his color."

The others nodded, impressed.

"What do others call your people?" Horse continued.

The oldest of the three, who had seemed the most dangerous, chuckled. "Some call us Ring-Noses," he indicated.

From his pack he drew out a slender ring of clamshell, or bone, and deftly inserted it through a hole in the septum of his nose!

"Do all your people wear these?" Red Horse asked,

trying to maintain his composure, as if he frequently saw people with rings through their noses.

"Not all . . . and not all the time. It is harder to eat. They are mostly for ceremonies."

Red Horse had also determined by this time that what had appeared to be a very intricate pattern of face painting, worn by all three, was actually permanent. He had seen tattooing before, but not to this extent or in such complicated, intricate patterns. This procedure was carried out, he had heard, by the process of rubbing dark pigments into tiny cuts in the skin. He did not pursue that topic. Another's religion is no one's concern.

He shared his own Creation story, of First Man, First Woman, and the log. He omitted the part about Fat Woman, thinking that the joke might be lost, somehow, in this strange and unfamiliar setting.

The next day at dawn the others departed, packing the meat behind their saddles. The man who had been so belligerent, he with the ring in his nose, had changed his attitude considerably. He was now the possessor of the medicine bag from the white bull and was beginning to gloat over this acquisition. He had inverted and carefully scraped the sac and stuffed it with dry grasses to retain its shape and allow it to dry. There would be ample time for tanning and curing later. He would undoubtedly spend the rest of his life telling of his prowess in obtaining this wonderful medicine bag.

"It is good to meet a great holy man," Ring-Nose signed in parting. "May our medicines continue to be strong, as they have been while we worked together."

Red Horse was amused. This was the man who, only a day ago, had threatened to kill him for his horse. Now the man was taking credit for the success of Red

Horse's quest. He was even more amused when he
noticed a quiet smile on the face of one of the younger
men. It was a covert thing, a smile of understanding.
The man said nothing, but their eyes met for a moment as they turned away. Red Horse realized that
the ring-nosed man must have something of a reputa-
tion among his own people for such illogical ideas and
actions. He wondered whether the other two men
would have risen to his, Red Horse's, defense, if the
confrontation had come to that. Well, no matter now.

The warriors mounted, and turned back toward him
for a moment.

"May your trail be easy," Red Horse signed.

"And yours, holy man," replied the man who had
smiled.

Ring-Nose was already kicking his horse into a trot,
as the others turned to follow.

Now he was alone, and the hard work was only
beginning. He had begun to dress the white skin already, scraping all fragments of flesh and fat from its
surface, so that it was nearly dry without spoiling.
There would be more work now, even harder. He
prepared the liver that he had saved, cooking and
crumbling it with a little water, then gradually kneading in the brains of the animal. He spent most of the
morning in preparing this paste and then began to rub
it into the flesh side of the skin. Through the rest of the
day he watched, sprinkling a little water on any area
that appeared to be drying too fast, kneading, pulling,
stretching, rubbing again.

Through the cooler night he slept, rising a time or
two to check the progress of curing. The next day he
carried the skin to a sapling he had selected. He bent
the little tree and tied it to provide a pole over which
to stretch and pull the curing hide, and began the

heaviest part of the work. At first he wondered if he could do the work alone. He had watched many times as two people, usually two women, pulled a skin back and forth across a pole, stretching and softening as the curing progressed. He had even assisted. But alone? His arms ached, and the sweat poured from his body. He would pause to rest, and begin again. He ate only a little, not wanting to spare the time from attending to this most important of tasks.

By the time shadows fell, purpling the canyon, the skin was nearly finished. He took some of the curing paste that he had saved and rubbed it into a stiff spot or two along the edge of the hide. He would work those spots out in the morning. Then he virtually collapsed into his sleeping robe, for the most restful, carefree night he had spent for many moons. He did not even dream.

It was a somewhat elaborate ceremony that Red Horse carried out the next morning, on the cliff's rim. He had climbed there in the gray light of the false dawn, to be ready. First the Song for Morning, to greet the dawn, and then his own prayerful song of thanksgiving for the success that had been his, in acquiring the white cape for the People. He held the cape aloft to catch the first rays of the sun and sacrificed bits of meat of the white bull in the ceremonial fire he had kindled, with grateful praise of whatever spirits had helped him. His heart was full.

Descending again to the canyon floor, he began his preparations to leave. The skin seemed dry enough, though he would continue checking it closely. It must not begin to heat in the warm sun of midday.

Thus far, he had done nothing with the horns of the bull. They would be needed to construct the horned headdress that would be used with the cape. But the horns were not subject to the spoilage that had endangered the white fur. Now that the skin was under control, he could divert his attention.

The horns were black and shiny, beautiful in themselves. They would grace the headdress nicely. He had hacked them free from the massive skull when he had opened it to obtain the brains for tanning. Now he trimmed and scraped the bony bases of each horn. They still required no immediate care but would be simpler to carry. Later, they could be scraped, polished, hollowed to reduce weight, and fastened to the cap that would form the headdress. Already, Horse was planning how best to cut and shape the skin, how to sew the most showy parts . . . ah, well, that would come later. Swallow would help.

Swallow. He missed her now. He had missed her all along, of course, since the day they parted. In the stress of his difficult days, he had wished for her help. The world had always seemed better when viewed from the comforting vantage point of her embrace.

But now, in this day of his success, how much more he wished for her, to share the triumph: his own, and the triumph of the People. They would celebrate the achievement by . . . but he must postpone such thoughts. The trail was long, the journey hard, until they would be together. And he must be on that trail. Nearly two moons had passed.

He drank deeply, filled his waterskins, and allowed the roan stallion to drink. Then he took the rein and led the horse up the path to the top of the cliff again. Checking all the ties and lashings, he swung to the animal's back and pointed north.

The horse seemed to sense that they were going home, stepping out with an eagerness he had not demonstrated in many days. Maybe it was only the rest and grazing that their few days at the canyon had afforded, but it seemed that the roan actually understood the situation and carried himself with pride. At least, Red Horse felt that he did.

They camped that night far from the canyon's rim. Red Horse sat staring into his little fire for a long time. He thought of Digging Owl, and the Hole-in-the-Earth. What a gift Owl had possessed, what insight, and what dedication. If instead he had been the one who was called upon to die for his people, Red Horse wondered, could he have done it?

It was over. He felt a deep sense of calm, but an exciting sort of calm, that made it difficult to sleep tonight. In the distance, a coyote cried to its mate, and the world was good.

22

>> >> >>

New Grass peered across the plain at the lone horseman. She had been watching for several days now, expecting him.

There had been the storm, which came sweeping across the earth with spears of lightning and the roll of drumming thunder. And the buffalo were moving, driven by an odd storm front that seemed to hover over the herd and drive it north. Buffalo should not be migrating now, not at this time of the year. Of course, the herds had not behaved normally for two seasons, because of the weather and the drought. That had been the reason for the quest of the two holy men. . . .

Aha! Of course, that must be it. Since they passed this way, there had been just about enough time. The two had wanted to find and bring back the buffalo, and now the buffalo had returned. Their mission must be complete, and she could expect their return. The re-

turn of one, anyway. The old woman had been shaken
by her premonition that one would die. She had seen
no more, and still did not know which one it had been,
but she was convinced that, when the time came, only
one would pass this way again.

As she thought about it, she became more certain
that they had had something to do with that strange
storm. It had been filled with fire and thunder and had
been much like her vision, in which she had glimpsed
death for one of the holy men. They had been skilled
medicine men, both of them. She could tell that. Possibly they had been gifted with the most powerful medicines she had ever seen. She had enjoyed their visit,
and the evening they spent together. It was good, to
share things of the spirit that were there, recognized
by all, yet remained unspoken. Such an opportunity
was rare, to share a time with even one such holy man.
And these two! The tall one on the fine horse . . .
such a figure of a man! He had said little of his vision,
but she could tell that it was deeply ingrained in his
life, a thing he would willingly give his life for. It must
have had to do with the restoration and return of the
buffalo.

The other man, the shorter, darker one, he too was
skilled, and he too was dedicated. His was a different
medicine but equally powerful. He had spoken more
of the legend that both their nations knew, that of the
hole in the ground from which the buffalo had come.
Both had seemed to feel that the herds might have
returned through the hole. Well, maybe so. She had
wondered that herself.

Of one thing, she was certain. If what was needed
was a ceremony to reopen the hole, either of the holy
men who had camped with her could have handled it.
And they had had a common goal, the buffalo's return.

Yet she had sensed that they were not totally in unison. Their communication, their trust in each other, had seemed not quite complete.

Now she had witnessed the return of the buffalo, driven by the storm. She was certain that the medicine of one or the other of her erstwhile guests was somehow responsible. Maybe the gifts of both, acting together. Anyway, it was good, the restoration of the way of things, the movements of the herds. The world felt better to her, better attuned now.

So she had waited, expecting the return of one or the other of the holy men, she knew not which one. She was relatively certain that there would be only one, for her death-vision was rarely wrong. It had happened too many times, through her lifetime, to take lightly.

Now came the expected traveler. She had spotted him about midmorning. At first she could not distinguish anything but a moving animal, nearly half a day's travel away on the flats that were her world. A buffalo, separated from the herd? She watched for a long time and could not tell, could not even tell whether the dark speck was moving. Finally she resorted to a trick she remembered from her childhood on the prairies. She took two small sticks and inserted them in the sand behind her lodge. Lying flat on the sand, she sighted across the two and carefully aligned them, moving the farther one until they rested exactly on the image of the distant creature in question. Then she rose and busied herself for a little while at other things, to return and sight again. Ah! Yes, the distant image had changed. It *was* moving, traveling almost directly toward her.

She sat up and used another device. She cupped her right hand, almost tight like a fist, and peered through the tunnel that it formed, closing her other eye. This shut out much of the extraneous light, allowing her to see the distant object more clearly. By midday, she could tell that the moving speck was a horse and rider. Unfortunately, by that time the shimmering heat of sun on sand was distorting the figure, so she abandoned watching, taking only a brief look from time to time, to measure the rider's progress.

It would be a long time yet before she could distinguish the color of the horse or any details about the rider. It was odd, she had always thought, that at a distance colors are all alike. A horse could be black or bay or gray or any other shade, and until it came within a few hundred paces, it was a neutral non-color. It was so in this case. She could not identify the man or the horse, even by color.

She grew impatient as time passed, curiosity gnawing at her, making her restless. This annoyed her, the inability to settle down to anything constructive. She paced and worried and wondered.

Finally, she recognized the roan stallion, not by his color but by his smooth, steady gait. Then it was easy to begin to put other observations together as the horse and rider came nearer—the tall way that the rider sat, straight-backed in the saddle, his easy sway with the rocking motion of the horse. So. It was the taller of the two, he of the Elk-dog People, who had survived. She was glad he was the one, though she felt sorrow for the other.

She could now begin to see that the pack behind his saddle was somewhat bulkier than she remembered. She wondered if he was bringing back the possessions of the dead man.

He rode straight up to her as she stood in front of her dwelling and, with the gentlest twitch of the rein, drew the roan to a stop. The horse gave a deep sigh and relaxed, knowing that the hard, hot journey was over for the day.

"*Ah-koh,* Mother," Red Horse greeted. "May I camp here tonight?"

"Welcome, holy man," she signed. "It is good."

The rider dismounted and took a few steps, shakily at first, to work the stiffness out of his leg muscles. It was only then that New Grass realized the nature of the bundle behind his saddle.

"Ah!" she gasped. "White? A white skin? Is it buffalo?"

"Yes, Mother. I had seen it in a vision. A very old medicine cape of my people."

"But this . . . this is not old," she protested.

He was busily stripping the packs and saddle from the horse's back, but paused to sign an answer.

"No. It was lost to us, many lifetimes ago. It fell to me to recover it."

"Then *that* was your mission? I knew there was something. And the other one . . . your companion . . . he is dead."

It was a statement, not a question. He looked at her strangely for a moment.

"You knew."

"Yes."

"You tried to tell us."

"Yes, but I knew it would happen anyway. I could not see which one."

He nodded. He took the bridle from the roan's head and turned him loose. The stallion trotted to an open space to roll luxuriously in the sand, while they watched.

"My mission was not finished," he observed.

"That is true. But I did not know of that part," she stated apologetically. "Anyway, it was to be."

She stood uncomfortably for a moment and then resumed the conversation, hesitantly.

"Holy man, would you . . . may I see the white cape?"

He hesitated a moment, and seemed to be considering.

"I am sorry." She interrupted his thoughts. "I have no right to ask of your medicine."

"No, no," he answered quickly. "It is not my medicine but that of my people. It will be used as a public ceremony, for all to see."

He untied the bundle and spread the white cape on the ground for her to see. Its whiteness was dazzling, the fur thick and soft.

"May I touch it?"

He laughed. "Of course. Your medicine has helped us, Mother."

She was excited at the privilege and touched the soft fur almost reverently.

"You have tanned it well. How will it be used?"

"A cape . . . we must make it when I reach my home."

He drew out the horns to show her and indicated how they would be fastened to a cap or headdress, to be worn with the cape. She nodded in understanding. Then an idea struck her.

"Holy man," she began, "I could help you. The headdress, the cape, could be finished in a day or two."

"No . . . my wife will help with that."

She tried to hide her disappointment. "But . . . think, holy man. You could join your people with the white cape complete. Its first viewing could be a ceremony, on your return. Your wife could then do other things. . . ."

She gave him a slightly suggestive look and saw that he was thinking of what other things a wife might devise on her husband's return.

"Yours is the design," she continued, "but I would be honored to help with such powerful medicine."

She could see that he was now thinking seriously about her offer. It would, of course, be a wonderfully spectacular ceremony, to unfurl the white cape in finished form on his return, not merely as a tanned skin. And any holy man knew well the value of showmanship.

At last, he chuckled. *"Aiee,* Mother, I am made to feel that you are right. You know of such things."

"I have watched such things for my whole life," she answered.

"Yes. But you also have a gift of the spirit."

"Sometimes more a curse than a gift," she reminded.

"Yes, that is true. You knew of Digging Owl. . . ."

"Yes, too bad. You mourned him?"

"I did. I sang our Song of Mourning."

"It is good. A brave man. . . . You think he knew?"

"Yes, Mother. I am made to think he planned it."

"Maybe. But now, let us eat. I have been cooking. Then you may tell me how you want the cape and headdress."

23

>> >> >>

"**Y**ou should pack it with the horns and the fur inside," the old woman indicated. "Then no one will see the value of such a wonderful thing."

The idea was good. Wrapped and lashed in this way, the white cape and its headdress appeared to be only another pack. It would not arouse the curiosity of anyone he chanced to meet on the trail. But Red Horse was amused at her solicitous advice. He had enjoyed the past two days, working together to fashion the cape that would become so important to the People.

These two, so different in all ways, had found a closeness of the spirit. Possibly it was because of the intensity of the gifts of spirit that both possessed. They still had very little spoken language in common, but had conversed much in signs.

"Here, let me help," New Grass signed, busily tucking in fringes of white fur. "Now, leave it like that, until you are home."

"You talk like my mother," he teased. He had found that she enjoyed this sort of teasing.

The leathery old face crinkled into a hundred lines of laughter around her eyes and cheeks. "Someone has to look after you," she retorted.

He smiled. "Mother, why are you out here?" he asked. "Have you no family?"

She brushed the question aside. "This is my lodge," she signed.

"But you are alone. What is your tribe?"

"Never mind. That is a story too long to tell, and you must travel."

He saw a sadness in her eyes that he did not understand, and knew that her life had been hard. He also felt, somehow, that this was a woman of the grassland, not the desert country. The way she used some of the hand signs, her facial features, her height, all said so.

An idea struck him, and he spoke impulsively.

"Mother, come with me, back to my people."

She smiled a sad little smile and shook her head.

"No, no. You are a good man, Red Horse, a holy man with great gifts of the spirit. If we had met when I was your age . . ." She looked at him flirtatiously. "But you were not born yet. It is my misfortune . . . and yours!"

Red Horse laughed. "No, Mother, I did not want to marry you."

Again, there was a hint of sadness in her face. "I know, my son. But this is my home. I will live out my days here, talking to travelers. It is what I have chosen."

He nodded. "It is yours to choose. I thank you for your help, Mother, and for the help of your medicine."

"It is good. I am glad, Red Horse, that you are the

one who survived. If I want to move, I will look for you among the Elk-dog People."

"Good. My lodge is yours."

He mounted and waved good-bye, then turned the stallion northward. He glanced back from time to time and could see the seated figure of the old woman, watching her desert domain . . . until the little hut became only a tiny toy in the distance.

It was several sleeps before he encountered another human being. It was at evening, as it had happened to him before. He looked up from preparing his fire, to find a party of mounted warriors watching him. He did not know how they had approached so quietly. He would not even have looked up, except that the roan had spoken to his brothers as they came near.

Quickly, Red Horse evaluated the situation. Six . . . no, seven men. Maybe a hunting party. Only then did he recognize the leader. Bow-Legs! These, then, were Owl's people.

"*Ah-koh,* Uncle," Horse greeted. "We meet again!"

The expression on the surly face did not change. "Where is Digging Owl?"

"Ah, he is dead," Horse signed.

"You killed him!" accused one of the young men, reaching for a weapon.

Bow-Legs stopped him with a wave of the hand and a terse command. He turned back to Horse.

"Is that true?"

Red Horse was astonished. "No! Of course not! Owl was my friend, and a great holy man."

"You saw him die?" demanded Bow-Legs.

"Yes . . . I was with him."

"You buried him?"

Aiee, this could be tricky. He must convince friends

and relatives of Digging Owl that he was not responsible and that he had acted honorably.

"I mourned him. . . . Come, camp with me, and I will tell you everything."

The men dismounted and busied themselves with caring for their horses, stripping packs and saddles, and selecting places to drop their belongings. Some began to gather fuel for the fire. One man, the one who had accused Horse of Owl's death, still glared with hate. He must watch that one, who seemed irrationally obsessed somehow. That man could be dangerous.

The party began to drift back toward the fire, and Bow-Legs approached Horse.

"That is Owl's brother," he indicated. "He brought this party to search. Be careful."

It was good of Bow-Legs to inform him, and Horse nodded in understanding.

"Thank you, Uncle. But I will tell all. You have found buffalo?"

"Yes. That is why Turtle expected his brother home. Owl's mission should have been over."

It was darkening now, and an evening chill fell across the plain. Red Horse realized that the summer was nearly gone. But now the warriors were seating themselves near the fire. He was in the position of storyteller, but never before had his ability been so challenged. If he was not convincing enough . . . *aiee,* was he to have come this far, only to fail because of a misunderstanding?

He thought of New Grass and remembered her warning as he and Digging Owl stopped on their quest. There had been no such warning about his homeward trail. Surely, the old woman's gift would have shown her. He felt a little more confidence. But now, they were waiting.

"My brothers," he began, "it is good to find you, that I may tell you of my friend, Digging Owl."

He glanced at the interested faces around the circle and was startled that there was still hatred in the eyes of Owl's brother. That one might be hard to convince.

"As you know," Horse went on, "the past two seasons have been dry and strange. The buffalo did not return."

There were nods around the circle, but only a look of impatience on the face of Turtle. Horse hurried on.

"My people suffered, as yours did," he continued. "Our holy men met together, to make medicine, and to question, to find a way to bring back the herds.

"I was given a vision, what I must do, and I started on my quest. Your brother too, Digging Owl, was given a vision-quest, one much the same as mine. We met and went on together."

"Go on with the story," interrupted Turtle. "We know all these things!"

"Of course, my brother," Horse hurried on. "As we traveled, your holy man and I became close friends. Our medicines were different, but they seemed to do well together. We finally reached the place that Digging Owl's vision had shown him: the Hole-in-the-Earth, where the buffalo were. There were hundreds, thousands of them. But . . . how to get them out? How to make such a herd start back out onto the plain? Our brother, Owl, had been given the answer.

"As you remember, a powerful part of Owl's medicine was the rain ceremony."

There were nods again.

"He had done this, once, when we were nearly dying of thirst, and brought rain. I saw that his medicine was one of great power. When we found the buffalo, he left me, without telling me what he was about to do, and danced his rain ceremony high on a cliff over-looking the hole."

It was fully dark now, lending to the aura of the storyteller. Red Horse took full advantage of the atmo-sphere to describe the coming of the rain, the crash of real-fire, the boom of Rain Maker's drum.

"Then the buffalo, startled by the noise and storm, began to run. Up, up and out of the hole, onto the plain, back into the world. It was as Digging Owl had planned it."

"Wait!" demanded Turtle. "Where were *you?*"

"*Aiee!* My brother, I was trapped, between the real-fire at the top of the cliff and the buffalo below. I climbed on a large rock, to avoid being trampled. Just then came a huge spear of real-fire, a loud crack! . . . My brothers, it was that spear that struck Digging Owl. I could smell the smoke of the Spirit World, as it opened for him. I saw him fall . . . then there was darkness."

There was complete silence as Red Horse paused a moment for effect: one, two, three heartbeats.

"When day came, I searched, but the buffalo had stampeded across the place, and now it ran with a flood. I could not find my brother Owl, so from the top of my rock I sang the Song of Mourning for a brave holy man who gave his life to bring back the buffalo."

It was quiet a little while, until Turtle rose.

"Why," he demanded, "would Digging Owl dance his ceremony on the cliff top, where real-fire would strike? Owl was not that stupid! You lie!"

Red Horse's heart was very heavy. He had spoken truth, and he was not believed. Would he now have to fight this man who claimed vengeance? All the others seemed to accept the story as he had told it.

"I think you killed him!" accused Turtle, drawing his knife.

Red Horse had a knife at his waist, but he waited a moment. If he drew the knife, the fight was on.

"Wait!" he signed. "What would that benefit me?"

Turtle paused, confused. He seemed uncertain, unable to answer this logic. Now Bow-Legs rose and stepped between the two. He spoke harshly to Turtle, who hesitated, then finally sheathed his knife, still unconvinced. Bow-Legs motioned for both men to sit down and then began to talk, using words and signs together so that Red Horse could understand.

"Turtle," he began, "I have met this holy man before, when your brother did. I did not trust him at first, but Digging Owl did. We shared his food and learned that he and Owl were on the same mission. It is as this man says. What good would it do him, for Owl to die?"

Turtle said nothing.

"Now, your question is good. Why would Digging Owl, who was not stupid, do a stupid thing like a dance on top of the cliff, to attract the lightning? I am made to think that that *is* why. He felt he must draw the real-fire, to bring the herd out of the hole. Right, holy man?"

He did not wait for an answer, but hurried on.

"For a man such as our brother Digging Owl, his life was a small thing to give for the return of the buffalo."

Red Horse was astonished. He had misjudged the wisdom of this man. Because he had seemed sullen and aggressive, Horse had assumed he was not very intelligent. And now the man's wisdom was saving his life.

"I have been made to think, Uncle, that it is as you

say," he signed. Then he turned to Turtle and continued. "My brother . . . brother of my friend . . . is this not like the way of Digging Owl?"

Turtle was thoughtful for a moment. "Yes," he nodded finally, "it may be as you say. Will you tell me more of your time together? Of my brother's last days?"

"It is good," announced Bow-Legs. "But now, let us eat. *We* have meat to share this time, holy man!"

24
>> >> >>

Swallow cut strips of meat and draped them over the rack of willow sticks to dry, then turned back to the buffalo haunch to cut more. The Fall Hunt had been good, and everyone had been working hard through the long days of the Moon of Hunting, to prepare meat for the winter. There would be no Moon of Starvation this year. The People were well fed, the children fat, and the women happy. The buffalo had returned.

But her heart was heavy, because her husband had not. When the wolves—the outriders who guarded the camp—had reported sighting a herd, Blue Swallow knew that Red Horse's mission was a success. She had run to the lodge of his parents to share the news. They had heard too, and White Fox was offering a prayer of thanksgiving.

Yet the days passed, and Red Horse did not return. The days of summer were over, and in the mornings there was a crisp feel of autumn in the air. Soon it would be the Moon of Falling Leaves. The People would be moving to winter camp. Swallow knew she could see to the transporting of the lodge and its contents. She had done so already when the bands had scattered for the summer after the Sun Dance. That was as it should be. Friends and relatives were well aware that their holy man was on a special mission, brought on by a vision back in the Moon of Roses. They had offered help quite freely.

When the buffalo returned, there was great rejoicing, as well as great feasting. Many hunters shared their kills with the family of the absent holy man.

"Red Horse has been successful," the other women told her. "The buffalo have returned. Now he will come home."

But still he had not returned. Swallow was still elated at the success of his quest, but a feeling of anxiety kept creeping in. She knew of the other part of his quest, that for the white bull, which most others did not. Had he not yet found the bull? Had that hunt gone wrong? Maybe . . . she dreaded to think such thoughts. Had he been forced to pay with his life for the return of the buffalo to the People? He would have hesitated not at all, she knew, if that were necessary.

She finished stripping meat that one of the hunters had left and sat to rest for a moment. The day was fading, and Sun Boy was painting the western sky as he prepared to go to his lodge for the night. The colors were brilliant, in reds and purples and yellows. Swallow decided to walk to the top of the little rise behind the camp. She did that sometimes when she wished to be alone to think, or merely to be alone with thoughts of Red Horse and how much she missed him. It was the longest that they had been apart since their marriage. He had been gone for the season, the summer before they were married, but that was different. They had not yet decided to wed, and both were living in the lodges of their parents. White Fox had been asked to guide the French party . . . *aiee,* what tales Horse had told her of *that* summer. He and his mother had accompanied White Fox and had seen many strange things. People whose eyes were blue, yet they could see . . . a man called Black Paint, because his skin was born with paint that could not be washed off . . . and women. . . . She had worried about that at the time.

Red Horse had assured her on his return that there had been none to compare to her. But he had told her, later, of the wantonness of the trader's wife, and the easy virtue of some of the women of tribes they had met along the northern river which the French called the Platte. He had told her he had not indulged in any dalliance with these women, and she believed him. Other than occasional teasing between them, about other women, there had been no mention and no cause for suspicion.

There still was none, except that he had been gone a long time. Swallow had made certain that her husband had much to remember during his absence, to make him hurry home. She was a little ashamed of her jealous distrust. She should not be concerned about other women, only about his life, she told herself again and again. But they had never been apart so long, and the nights were growing cool. She missed the warmth of his body in the sleeping robes.

She reached the top of the hill and watched the shadows lengthen across the golden plain. The evening was still, and she could hear the coming alive of the night creatures. A hunting owl called his hollow cry in the oak thicket below the camp. A coyote called from a distant ridge.

Two of the wolves, or outriders, who constantly circled the camp to give warning or information of any approach, were coming in from the southwest. They usually rode two by two . . . no, there were *three* men. She jumped to her feet, shading her eyes against the setting sun. The three were actively gesturing as they rode, an animated conversation. Could it be?

One of the riders kicked his horse into a lope toward the camp. Swallow eagerly watched the others for a moment. One carried packs, as if he had been traveling. . . . Yes! Surely that was the roan stallion on which he rode, the prized buffalo horse of Long Lance.

She was running, now, to meet the horsemen. The messenger, who was nearest, veered aside toward her.

"Swallow!" he called. "Your husband is home!"

She waited, now, as the others quickened their pace and approached. Red Horse leaped from the horse and gathered her in his embrace. *Aiee,* it was good.

The celebration that night was one to be long remembered among the People. White Fox and South Wind helped with the preparation, and a great story fire was held. Red Horse related all his adventures: of the crossing of the desert; of Digging Owl, the holy man whose ceremony could call up Rain Maker himself. The audience gasped in awe at his description of the Hole-in-the-Earth. They were spellbound by the tale of Owl's death, for the purpose of causing the buffalo to return. But the best was yet to come.

"Now, my brothers," Red Horse finally said with much dramatic emphasis, "my quest had another purpose, unknown to you. I had a vision which called me.

You have heard, maybe, of a time in our past, when our holy man, White Buffalo, was keeper of a white cape. It was a thing of great beauty and of very strong medicine."

There were a few nods, by some of the older members of the tribe.

"I was made to think," Red Horse continued, "that its loss, long ago, was a hurt to the People . . . to our things of the spirit. Maybe this had caused our misfortune, the past seasons. I was made to think that I should go and recover it."

"Into the hole?" someone whispered incredulously to his neighbor.

Now White Fox began to beat a slow, rhythmic cadence on the dance drum, and Red Horse stepped into the darkness behind a nearby lodge for a moment. Swallow placed the horned headdress on his head and helped him tie the cape. Then he danced back out into the circle of firelight, swaying in the ponderous gait of the buffalo. There was a gasp of approval that became almost a roar. Surely, this was one of the greatest of holy men their nation had ever seen. And surely, good times were ahead. Had it not already begun?

It was some time later that Red Horse and Swallow lay snuggled in the sleeping robes. The camp was quiet now. The buzz of human activity had tapered to an almost inaudible hum. Even the night sounds were muted. Somewhere at the opposite side of the camp, a dog barked, and someone yelled sleepily at it.

Neither of them were ready to sleep. There was too much excitement, besides that afforded by their reunion. That, of course, had been wonderful. But now they lay in each other's arms, as if their hunger for this could never be satisfied. For a long time they said very little.

"I am so proud," Swallow whispered. "Horse, the white cape . . . so beautiful! I am made to think that this is the most important day in all the life of the People."

"Maybe," he agreed. "I still cannot believe it, Swallow. But *aiee*, I am glad to be home!"

"You missed me, then?" she teased. "I thought maybe you were too busy."

He held her closer. "One does not become that busy," he growled in her ear.

She pulled away from him. "No . . . wait, Horse, tell me seriously. I asked you once before, when you returned, if there were other women."

"When I went with my father, before?"

"Yes. Now, I ask you again, of this time. You were gone a long while."

Red Horse thought a moment. He had faced death in many forms and might have faced the choice she mentioned. But he had not. It was amusing, now she had him safely back, that this was her concern.

"Well," he said seriously, "there was one woman, she who helped me to sew the headdress and the cape. I asked her to come home with me, but she would not."

There was only a short pause before her fingers dug into his ribs, in the vulnerable places she loved to tickle. He squealed involuntarily, and they rolled together, giggling and tickling, like happy children.

The quest was over, and he was home.

GENEALOGY

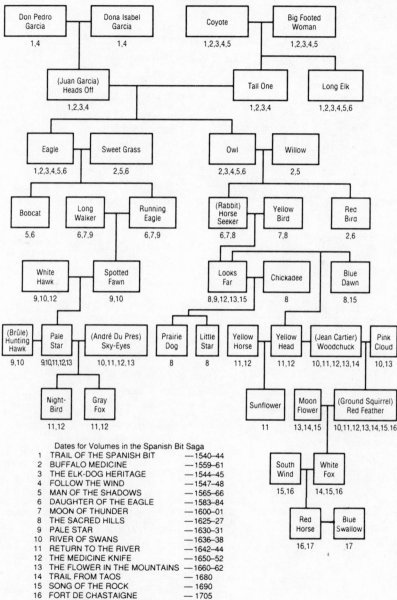

Dates for Volumes in the Spanish Bit Saga

1 TRAIL OF THE SPANISH BIT   —1540–44
2 BUFFALO MEDICINE   —1559–61
3 THE ELK-DOG HERITAGE   —1544–45
4 FOLLOW THE WIND   —1547–48
5 MAN OF THE SHADOWS   —1565–66
6 DAUGHTER OF THE EAGLE   —1583–84
7 MOON OF THUNDER   —1600–01
8 THE SACRED HILLS   —1625–27
9 PALE STAR   —1630–31
10 RIVER OF SWANS   —1636–38
11 RETURN TO THE RIVER   —1642–44
12 THE MEDICINE KNIFE   —1650–52
13 THE FLOWER IN THE MOUNTAINS —1660–62
14 TRAIL FROM TAOS   —1680
15 SONG OF THE ROCK   —1690
16 FORT DE CHASTAIGNE   —1705
17 QUEST FOR THE WHITE BULL   —1710

Dates are only approximate, since the People have no written calendar.
Characters in the Genealogy appear in the volumes indicated.

Don Coldsmith was born in Iola, Kansas, in 1926. He served as a World War II combat medic in the South Pacific and returned to his native state where he graduated from Baker University in 1949 and received his M.D. from the University of Kansas in 1958. He worked at several jobs before entering medical school: he was a YMCA group counselor, a gunsmith, a taxidermist, and for a short time a Congregational preacher. In addition to his private medical practice, Dr. Coldsmith is a staff physician at Emporia State University's Health Center, teaches in the English Department, and is active as a freelance writer, lecturer, and rancher. He and his wife of twenty-six years, Edna, have raised five daughters.

Dr. Coldsmith produced the first ten novels in "The Spanish Bit Saga" in a five-year period; he writes and revises the stories first in his head, then in longhand. From this manuscript he reads aloud to his wife, whom he calls his "chief editor." Finally the finished version is skillfully typed by his longtime office receptionist.

Of his decision to create, or re-create, the world of the Plains Indian in the sixteenth and seventeenth centuries, the author says: "There has been very little written about this time period. I wanted also to portray these native Americans as human beings, rather than as stereotyped 'Indians.' That word does not appear anywhere in the series —for a reason. As I have researched the time and place, the indigenous cultures, it's been a truly inspiring experience for me."